FINDER

DOVE SEASON

ROBIN BRANDE

RYER PUBLISHING

FINDER
(Dove Season)
By Robin Brande

Published by Ryer Publishing
www.ryerpublishing.com
Copyright 2025 by Robin Brande
www.robinbrande.com
Cover art by yurok.a/Deposit Photos
Cover design by Ryer Publishing
All rights reserved.
Print ISBN: 978-1-952383-26-7
Ebook ISBN: 978-1-952383-00-7

ALSO BY ROBIN BRANDE

<u>Dove Season Universe</u>

Dove Season

Finder

Seeker

Believer

Maker

Explorer

<u>Winnie Parsons Mysteries</u>

The Genius Track

A Man of Appetites

A Drop of Sweat

The Long Gray Hook

The Slip of a Rib

<u>Parallelogram Quartet</u>

Into the Parallel

Caught in the Parallel

Seize the Parallel

Beyond the Parallel

<u>Young Adult</u>

Evolution, Me & Other Freaks of Nature

Fat Cat

Doggirl

Replay

<u>Bradamante Saga</u>

Book of Earth

Book of Water

<u>Romance</u>

Love Proof

Freefall

Heart of Ice

Fire and Ice

<u>Collections</u>

The Love of a Good Dog

Mountain Tough

The Miraculous Unknown

<u>Self-Help</u>

What If You're Doing It Right?

What If You're Doing It Right? For Teens

CONTENTS

FINDER

CORTEZ 1964

1

———

Travis Baird scrambled up the loose dirt incline in the light of a waning moon. His brown leather everyday shoes weren't suited. He should have bought outdoor boots in town, but he'd been in too much of a hurry after the call this morning from Dr. Linsk. *Get out there now, Travis. Be in position before it's dark.*

Travis's white Rambler station wagon made the trip from Fort Collins to Cortez, Colorado in about ten hours with four stops for gas. Travis's wife, Rosie, had the foresight to pack him three ham and cheese sandwiches and a thermos of coffee before he left, and he only wished she'd packed more. He didn't have time for dinner. His stomach was rumbling.

It was his first time out in the field. Alan Mayner was

usually the one sent out, but Alan was in the hospital with appendicitis. The job fell to Travis.

He needed to get it right. Dr. Linsk was going to hire only one of the biology post-docs to help him with his work as an advisor for the Agency, and Travis needed it to be him. He believed in the mission. And he had a wife and new baby girl to support.

Travis's foot slipped on the dirt. He dug in with his fingers and kept scrambling upward. He wished he could see the terrain better, but he couldn't risk his flashlight. He didn't want to draw any more attention to his presence than he had to.

Information about the UAOs—the unconventional aerial objects—sometimes came in hot on the roar of a rumor. But sometimes, like now, it trickled down slowly, until by the time Dr. Linsk got word of it, the sighting was already over a week old.

Apparently there was a lot of talk among the locals, but nothing had made the Cortez paper yet. The sheriff had discouraged letting the story out. Instead he asked around discreetly with his counterparts in other areas who had faced similar problems. Other sightings. Even a purported crash near Horsetooth Reservoir.

Sheriff Hoyt took their advice and called Dr. Linsk in the biology department at Colorado State University directly. That was good. It meant word might not have reached the Agency yet.

Dr. Linsk didn't want anyone in the Agency to hear

about it until he sent one of his own to check it out. If it was only a hoax, he wouldn't bother any of his superiors with it. He'd forward the information to the national hotline set up for kooks and frauds and be done with it.

But if it was real. The Agency needed to lock it down right away.

The fact that more than a few locals knew about it, that was what worried Travis. He didn't want to meet up with any curiosity seekers who could jeopardize the integrity of the scene.

If there even would be a scene tonight. He'd have to wait and see.

Everyone used to think the visitations were one-offs. A sighting in Utah or Nevada or New Mexico near one of the military bases. The cigar-shaped crafts, visible even in daylight, that seemed to create their own misty clouds around them. The silvery disks that peeled off the main crafts and then darted at unlikely speeds, evading any attempts to shoot them down.

There had been a visitation out at sea just a month ago. A hundred sailors stood on the deck of a Navy ship and stared at the red and white lights that flicked in and out directly above them for almost an hour.

Observing. Us observing them, them observing us.

Then the lights jetted off so impossibly fast it was as if they disappeared from the sky. The U.S. military didn't have aircrafts that moved like that. As far as they knew, no one else in the world did either.

But the ocean sightings were someone else's territory. Dr. Linsk's was Colorado.

Travis finally topped the ridge. He could see only dark shapes in front of him, trees and low scrub faintly lit by the weak moon draped with clouds.

He walked forward slowly, quietly, listening for any sound of voices. He appeared to be alone. Maybe the locals had gotten tired of waiting. Or maybe it was the cold. Watching for alien spaceships was a lot more appealing on a mild night.

Travis found the trunk of some kind of evergreen tree and sat with his back against it.

He looked up at the sky and waited.

What happened in New Hampshire last fall changed what they all thought they knew.

These visitations weren't one-offs after all. Not necessarily. A husband and wife, the Fullers, were driving home from a party one night on the isolated dirt road that led back to their farm, when suddenly their truck lifted off of the road.

Just rose into the air several feet. Not because it went over a bump or for any other natural reason. The couple had driven that same road a hundred times, and it was always as straight and solid as the Fullers themselves. But now they were suspended in the air, lifted by some unseen force. Mrs. Fuller screamed. Mr. Fuller might have, too.

The truck floated forward about a quarter of a mile,

then bounced back down to the road. Mr. Fuller pressed his foot hard against the gas, trying to outrun whatever just happened, but then the truck floated up again and the two of them clutched each other and shrieked.

Mr. Fuller stuck his head out the driver's side window and looked above them. A round object, flat on top with a sort of dome in the center of the bottom, hovered above them, an eerie blue light shining down from it onto the Fullers' truck.

The truck bounced down again. This time the Fullers were silent.

Mr. Fuller drove slowly, carefully, while he whispered urgently to his wife about what he saw.

"No, don't look!" he shouted, but too late. Mrs. Fuller stuck her head out to see.

The blue light hit her straight in the face. Mrs. Fuller howled with pain. Her eyes felt like someone had stuck them with burning pokers straight from a fire.

"I can't see! I can't see!"

Mr. Fuller turned the truck around and raced his wife back to town. The unconventional aerial object, whatever it had been, disappeared and left them alone.

The ophthalmologist who was called to the hospital said he'd never seen injuries like that in all his thirty-four years of practice.

The skin around Mrs. Fuller's eyes was so swollen he could barely pry them open even a little to look.

When he was finally able to shine a light on them, he

said her pupils looked like blood-filled marbles. They took two weeks to return to normal. Mrs. Fuller was blind that whole time. They weren't sure she'd get her sight back, but she did.

And then the Fullers, intrepid husband and wife that they were, spent the next seven weeks driving up and down that same dark, lonely road hoping it might happen again.

It did. One night around midnight they felt the familiar lift again of their truck. This time both of them had the sense to keep their heads inside.

They gradually started telling friends and family. More people began driving the no-longer-lonely road.

Four more people met with the mysterious craft and had their vehicles plucked off the ground.

And that's when the Agency sent out a new directive to all its teams urging them to be patient and send someone to stick around known sighting locations to see if it might happen there again.

The glowing white UAO here in Cortez had been seen by multiple witnesses a week ago. They said it descended toward the ridge with a strange jerking motion and then settled there for over an hour.

The next morning Sheriff Hoyt found indentations that might have been from the base of the craft.

All the vegetation around those indentations had been burned in a perfect circle ten feet around.

Like maybe a craft had touched down or lifted off.

Locals talked about coming up here the day after and scooping up handfuls of the alien dirt to keep for themselves. They started showing it around. More people climbed the ridge to collect jars of the dirt.

Travis had no hope that by now there would still be any samples worth collecting.

He would have to wait for a second visitation.

2

When Travis first told Rosie the kinds of projects he was working on, she covered her mouth and laughed.

He didn't care, he loved her laugh.

He had been courting her for several months, although he was so shy and unskilled at it, she probably didn't realize it for most of that time. Tuesdays through Saturdays, the days she worked as a waitress at the Sunshine Coffee Shop, he stopped in every single morning on his way to campus for a cup of black coffee and an order of buttered toast.

It was an expensive habit, one he really couldn't afford with the pittance he made as a lab assistant to Dr. Linsk, but he'd rather skimp on other expenses than give up that one. It was the best part of his day.

Rosie had wide, expressive brown eyes and a beautiful, ruby-lipped smile. She had long curly brown hair that she wore pulled back into a thick ponytail. She smelled like apricots, which he learned later was her favorite scent. She had an aunt who made homemade apricot lotions and apricot jam and often sent Rosie some of both.

Rosie always looked cheerful, even on the mornings when the coffee shop seemed overrun. She didn't get flustered. Travis liked that about her. He started thinking early on that he would like to marry a woman like that.

Then he realized what he really meant was to marry her.

It took him four months to build up the courage to ask her out.

They went to Brusco's, the Italian place, and over plates of spaghetti and meatballs they finally got to have a longer conversation than just the usual *How are you today?* and *Can you believe this rain?*

Travis learned that Rosie wanted to be a nurse, but she needed to save money for nursing school first, since her parents couldn't afford it.

He told her about wanting to be a scientist since he was a kid. How he used to study insects and birds in his back yard. Some of his fellow students wanted to use their PhDs to become professors, but all Travis ever wanted to do was research.

"What kind of research?" Rosie asked.

He wasn't really supposed to talk about it, but he did.

"Martian biology," he said.

That's when Rosie covered her mouth and laughed.

Travis was quick to attribute the idea to his doctoral advisor, Dr. Linsk, so Rosie wouldn't think Travis had just made it up on his own.

"There are pictures taken from some of the telescopes," Travis said. "We can actually see changes on the surface of Mars at different times of the year. We think it might be plants changing in whatever seasons they have up there. And if there are plants, there might be other kinds of life, too."

"Like… Martians?" Rosie asked.

"We would call them that," Travis said. "But we don't know what they look like yet."

Rosie looked at him with a mixture of amusement and doubt.

"We actually get funding from the Department of Defense," Travis said, hoping that would make the work sound more impressive and not just like a Saturday afternoon science fiction movie.

"Why would they do that?" Rosie asked, swishing her garlic bread through the leftover marinara sauce on her plate.

"Because we have to be ready," Travis said. "In case we need to go to Mars or some other planet some day. Or if…" He hesitated, swallowed. He really wasn't supposed to talk about this. "Or if they come here."

Rosie laughed again, but uncertainly this time. She tilted her head at him. "Tell the truth."

Travis leaned forward across the red-checkered table-cloth. He could smell the apricot on Rosie's skin.

"They've already been here," he whispered. "In 1947. A spaceship crashed in New Mexico. My professor has samples from one of the bodies."

Rosie's round eyes grew even rounder. "No, you're fooling. Stop it."

"I'm not fooling," he said. "I'm dead serious. You can't tell anyone. I'm not supposed to tell you."

After dinner they walked a bit on the street where Rosie lived. Travis had brought her home, but they weren't ready to be done with the date.

He told her all about Dr. Linsk's work for the defense department before Travis ever became his student. Then in 1962, when Travis was just beginning his PhD studies, a representative of the Agency came to see Dr. Linsk about doing more specialized work.

President Kennedy was going to make a speech in a few weeks, the representative said. The President was going to tell the world we were sending men to the moon.

Before any of that happened, the government needed to make sure it was safe.

They had reason to worry it wasn't. He told Dr. Linsk about the crashed spaceship from 1947. "It was right near one of our top-secret weapons installations," the man said. "That wasn't a coincidence."

No one knew where the spaceship came from, but "It wasn't from New Jersey," he said. Before President Kennedy sent any of our boys up into outer space, the government needed to know what else might be up there with them.

The man from the Agency said there were samples from the crash, "artifacts," he called them, stored at various military bases around the country. If Dr. Linsk wanted to become involved, the Agency would send over some artifacts in a few days.

Travis didn't know about any of that at the time. All he knew was one morning Dr. Linsk approached him in the lab and handed him a petri dish. Inside was a pale, rubbery-looking scrap of what looked like a blister you might get on your heel.

"Tell me what this is made of," Dr. Linsk said.

Travis thought it was an impromptu test.

He worked on it all day and into the night. By the next morning, exhausted and bleary-eyed, he had to confess to Dr. Linsk that he'd failed. He couldn't identify a single component of the blister, no matter how many different tests he tried to run.

Instead of looking disappointed, Dr. Linsk seemed delighted. He clapped his hand against Travis's back and told him to go home and get some rest.

In time he invited Travis, on a trial basis, to help him with some of the Agency's various projects.

Travis was excited about the work. He wanted to make a difference. He wanted to protect this world. And that might mean finding out whether beings from Mars or Venus or some other planet were spying on us and meant us harm.

"You're scaring me," Rosie said after he told her all that. She paused in their stroll along her street and huddled against him in the warm June air.

Travis felt as natural as he ever had putting his arm around her and gathering her in close.

When she lifted her face to his, he knew it was time to kiss her.

It took him five more months to save up for the smallest diamond ring. After Thanksgiving dinner with her parents and little brother, Travis asked Rosie to take another walk.

On the same street where he had first kissed her, in the exact same spot, he got down on one knee and proposed. Rosie covered her mouth and cried. Then she laughed and said yes.

Three days later President Kennedy was shot and killed.

Maybe, in a different kind of world, Rosie would have wanted a traditional wedding.

But life was short and love was too important to wait. They married just two weeks later.

The following September, just a month ago now, Travis and Rosie welcomed their baby girl. They named her Caroline, after the President's daughter.

On the cold hilltop near Cortez, his hands buried under his armpits to keep them warm, Travis thought of his two precious girls home waiting for him as he stared at the hazy stars.

3

"You want to go to Baxters," Sheriff Hoyt told Travis the following morning. "Get yourself some proper gear."

Travis showed up for their meeting wearing his everyday clothes: khaki cotton trousers, scuffed loafers, a light brown corduroy jacket over a dark brown sweater Rosie had packed him against the chill.

"Set to snow tonight or tomorrow," Sheriff Hoyt warned him. "I don't want to have to carry you down dead."

"Isn't it early for snow?" Travis asked. It was only the second week in October.

"Won't be the first time," Sheriff Hoyt said.

Travis discussed with the sheriff the various

witnesses who had seen the lights up on the ridge. He made a list with their names and addresses.

"That Parnell," Sheriff Hoyt said, referring to a rancher outside Cortez who was one of the first to call it in. "He's solid. No drinking, a straight shooter. Might want to talk to him first. Get the lay of the land."

Travis stopped in to Baxters first to buy thermal underwear and wool socks. Even though he assumed Dr. Linsk would put in for reimbursement from the government, Travis was afraid to overspend.

The truth was he'd rushed out of his house the previous morning not only without proper boots, but also without a proper winter coat. He needed both if it really was going to snow. At the last minute he threw in heavy gloves, too.

Wincing as he did it, Travis forked over the cash to the Baxters' cashier. He made sure to get a receipt. Then to compensate for his extravagance, he picked up two jelly donuts at a coffee shop nearby, planning on eating one of them as his lunch.

He gassed up the used but reliable Rambler station wagon and drove out to Bart Parnell's place.

4

Outside the town of Cortez the houses dwindled into long stretches of fenced pasture land. Horses grazed in twos and threes on the golden and russet grasses, their tails swishing away whatever flies were still lingering past summer.

At this elevation fall was just taking hold, and all the aspens along the two-lane were showy yellow with a few reds. Travis took his time. The drive was soothing to his eyes.

Behind the pastures rose hills of varying heights, and beyond them the more serious mountains. The ridge where Travis had sat in the cold and dark for most of the night was directly behind Bart Parnell's ranch. Travis turned left off the pavement onto the dirt road leading to Parnell's place.

He drove past a neat white wooden fence line. He counted eight horses grazing. Ahead was a modest-looking two-story house with brown wooden siding and red trim around the windows.

Travis parked the Rambler. He'd called ahead so Bart Parnell would expect him. As soon as Travis opened the car door, two Golden Retrievers raced to receive him, wildly barking and wagging their tails.

"If they bite you," called the man coming out the screen door, "you'll be the first one."

The rancher was taller than Travis by several inches, but slightly stooped in the way tough old men could be. Maybe from too many injuries over the years around livestock or the ranch's heavy machinery, or maybe just from slouching long hours every day in the saddle.

His handshake was firm. He looked at Travis with a certain amount of suspicion.

"How old are you?" Parnell asked him.

"Twenty-five, sir."

"And you say you're a scientist?"

"Yes, sir." Travis's voice had a slight break, out of nerves, making him sound like a boy just hitting puberty.

To back up his claim, he handed Bart Parnell one of the stiff white embossed business cards furnished by the Agency to Dr. Linsk.

Scientific Consultant, it said. *United States*. Nothing specifying what aspect of the United States was employing him.

On this and the four other cards in Travis's wallet, Dr. Linsk's name had been crossed out and Travis's name written in by Rosie's neat hand.

"Well, come on in," Bart Parnell said, gesturing for him to follow into the house.

It was an orderly place with a wide wooden porch in front. Two rocking chairs sat near the screened door, and beside the furthest one were two old pieces of light blue carpeting that looked like they had been cut to size with a knife.

The two Golden Retrievers accompanied Travis up onto the porch, then settled on their respective carpets to await any further intruders.

Travis stepped into the house. In front of him was a comfortable looking living room with a couch and a recliner and a television set in the corner. A fireplace along the far wall still gave off some heat from a few residual orange coals.

To the right, through an open doorway, was a bright kitchen with a window set over the sink. A middle-aged woman with her gray hair rounded back in a bun stood washing dishes there, elbow-deep in soapy water.

She turned at the sound of the screen door slapping closed and came out wiping her hands on her apron.

"My wife, Ellen," Parnell said, handing her the embossed card to look over.

"Travis Baird," she read.

"Yes, ma'am."

"Hungry, Travis?" she asked.

"'Course he's hungry," Parnell said. "Look at him."

Travis felt a fleeting embarrassment. He knew the polite thing was to turn the offer down. But his belly wasn't interested in polite. The house smelled of sausage and coffee, and he wanted both of those very much.

"Yes, ma'am," he answered. "Whatever it is smells too good to pass up."

Travis and Bart Parnell sat at a six-chaired dining table between the kitchen and the living room. The wood surface of the table looked scratched and pitted after many years of use.

Mrs. Parnell brought Travis a steaming cup of black coffee with a little pitcher of milk. "More, dear?" she asked her husband. He nodded and told her thank you.

There was a courtliness to their relationship that Travis found appealing. He could imagine still speaking to Rosie just like this when they were both the Parnells' age.

Soon Mrs. Parnell returned with coffee for her husband and a plate of heaven for Travis. Her homemade buttermilk biscuits were soft and thick, and smothered in warm sausage gravy that must have just come off of the stove. Travis took a moment to breathe in the smell and appreciate the deep dark flavors.

He was a quarter through the meal before he forced himself to pause and say something to Mrs. Parnell, who still stood near her husband's chair.

"These are the best biscuits and gravy I've ever had," Travis said, and he meant it.

Rosie was an excellent cook, but even she was the first to say that her mother was even better. Cooking was clearly another one of those skills that improved in people over time.

Mrs. Parnell beamed. She came over and gave Travis a pat on the shoulder. "You two talk now," she told her husband. "I've got plenty to do."

Bart Parnell sipped his coffee while Travis devoured the rest of his meal. Then, slightly abashed by how hungry he had been, Travis set aside the plate to get to work.

He opened his battered leather briefcase and pulled out a notebook and a pen.

Travis began with basic preliminary questions the way Dr. Linsk taught him, but Bart Parnell soon grew impatient and broke in.

"It was a spaceship," the rancher said. "No question in my mind."

Travis's heart picked up speed.

"Why do you say that, sir?"

"Ever fly a plane, son?" Parnell asked.

"No, sir."

"I did," he said. "Nineteen forty-two to forty-five. I was an old man compared to the other boys, but I had some experience flying when I was younger and I was still fit, so the Army put me to use."

Travis always liked to hear his own father talk about the war, even though he hoped he never had to see one himself.

"I've seen the way planes fly," Bart Parnell said. "That thing was no plane."

"Why do you say that?"

"It was *fast*," he said. "Unbelievably fast. It was like a firefly the way it could flit from one place to another." He flashed the fingers of his right hand to demonstrate, out in, out in.

"What color was the light?" Travis asked.

"White. Pure white against a black sky. When it kept going on, I went into the house and got my binoculars. Ellen came out and watched for a while. You can ask her."

"What shape was it?" Travis asked.

Parnell held up his slightly crooked pinky. "Upright. Like a rocket. You tell me, young man, was that one of ours?"

"No, sir," Travis said. "I don't think so."

"I don't either," said Parnell. "The Army isn't flying rockets here in Montezuma County. Besides, rockets don't move that way. They go up, they come down. They don't jerk around in the sky. And rockets don't land the way this one did."

"How's that?" Travis asked.

"Like a kitten," Bart Parnell said. "Soft-pawed. Came in hard, I thought it would crash, but then it stopped dead in the air right above the ground and just—" He pursed his lips and kissed the air. "Soft and sweet. Never seen anything like it."

Travis wrote his notes as fast as his hand allowed. He wanted to use all of Bart Parnell's descriptions.

"What happened after that?" Travis asked.

"Nothing," Parnell said. "I glassed it for another hour at least. I handed the binoculars off to Ellen every now and then so she could watch while I rested my eyes."

Travis would need to get a statement from her, too.

"Then when it was my turn again," Parnell said, "it suddenly took off, no warning. Rose about ten feet, that was all. Flit, zip, gone."

Flit, zip, gone, Travis wrote.

"Could you hear anything?" he asked. He could see the ridge now out the Parnells' living room window. Close enough that some sound might carry.

"Not a thing," Parnell said. "It was just like someone sneaked in and turned out the light."

5

On his way back to town Travis ate from a paper napkin filled with sugar cookies Mrs. Parnell had insisted on sending along.

It was after one o'clock. Travis had been out at their ranch several hours.

He still had eight more people he wanted to interview today. The eight Sheriff Hoyt thought had the clearest view of the craft—the *spaceship*, Bart Parnell came right out and called it—and would be the most reliable witnesses.

But Travis also wanted a chance to clear his mind. To let what he had heard from Mr. and Mrs. Parnell settle like sand that had been stirred up in a container of water.

Travis had read dozens of reports—maybe even a hundred by now—since he began working with Dr.

Linsk on the Agency projects. The details varied, but overall the stories were the same: ordinary people seeing lights, seeing shapes in the sky that moved unlike anything the U.S. or any other country had designed yet or built.

So what did it mean? What were they and where were they from? Could Dr. Linsk or any other scientist really say for sure?

Travis glanced at the other item besides the sugar cookies that the Parnells had sent him away with.

This one was wrapped in an old towel Mrs. Parnell said she wouldn't miss. It rested on top of Travis's brief-case on the passenger seat. It was too bulky to fit in the case.

"Found this the next day when I went up there," Bart Parnell said. "You're the scientist, see what you think."

Parnell had climbed up the ridge, just like Travis did, to see if there was anything to find. This was before word got around and people were going up with shovels and pails to gather some of what they were calling the alien dirt.

But what Bart Parnell found was something solid. Several of them, in fact, laid out around the rim of the burned out circle.

"I probably should have left them," he said as he carried out the collection and lined them up on the dining room table. "Not sure why I didn't. Maybe I thought kids would get them or something and they wouldn't respect what they had."

Travis picked up the smallest rock.

It was about six inches long and surprisingly light, like balsa wood. He turned it in his hand to see the holes along one of the edges. They looked like air pockets, the kind you'd see if you bit a malted milk ball in half.

"The other rocks outside the circle were all brown, just like you'd expect," Parnell said. "It was just the ones inside that had colors."

There were twelve rocks of various sizes laid out on the table, from the six-inch one to a lumpen mass about a foot across. All of them were a sickly shade of green.

The one Travis held in his hand was shaped like a small human.

A band of muted yellow ran across the figurine's open arms. The green body tapered off into footless legs. The head was slightly squared on top, like the figure might be wearing a crown or a square helmet.

Travis said nothing as he examined each of the rocks in turn.

Ellen Parnell was back with iced tea and a batch of the sugar cookies just warm from the oven. She stood beside her husband and looked down at the display.

"It's something," she said.

"It's something," Parnell agreed.

Each rock was deceptively light. Travis gripped one of them too hard and felt part of the brittle structure crumbling in his hand. He quickly set the rock back on the table.

"Ever seen that?" Bart Parnell finally asked him.

"No, sir," Travis lied. "Never."

He cleared his throat. His heart was thumping inside his chest. He felt scared all of the sudden, even though intellectually he knew the rocks probably couldn't hurt him.

He picked up the human-shaped figurine again. The open arms looked welcoming, almost loving. Inviting someone in for a hug.

"I don't mind you taking one of the others with you," Bart Parnell said, "but we'd like to keep that one."

Travis nodded. He returned the little human to the table and picked up one of the more lumpen rocks. He could hold it one-handed with his fingers stretched out.

As he shifted it in the light coming from the chandelier overhead and the living room window behind him, he could see pockets of white on the rock that almost looked like standing water. He ran the fingers of his opposite hand over them just to confirm they were actually dry.

He held it up to his nose and sniffed. "Scientists forget they have noses," Dr. Linsk was known to say. "Use all your senses before you go straight to a microscope."

The rock smelled unremarkable. Just a rock, nothing more.

Travis glanced up at Bart Parnell before testing it one

more way. He licked his finger, then swiped it across the green surface. Then he tentatively touched his finger to his tongue.

"Good Lord," Parnell said.

Travis hastily wiped his finger against his pants. "Nothing," he reported in what he hoped was an authoritative-sounding voice. As though scientists licked specimens all the time.

Mrs. Parnell had gone away and returned with an old light blue bath towel. Travis set his treasure inside it and she carefully closed the cloth around it.

Travis felt anxious now. Unnerved. In a hurry to leave this place.

To do what next, he didn't know. But somehow he couldn't relax anymore and stay.

But he knew Dr. Linsk would flay him if Travis didn't bring back pictures of every rock. He went out to the Rambler and got his camera and came back and did what he should.

Mrs. Parnell packed him a napkin full of warm cookies and Travis was soon treading across the wooden porch again. The Golden Retrievers had escorted him out and back for the camera, and now they escorted him again. Bart Parnell came this time, too.

When they reached the car the two men stopped and shook hands. Travis avoided Parnell's gaze at first, nervous about revealing his own nerves.

"Do me a favor," the rancher said.

Travis had to look at him. "Yes, sir?"

"Call me when you figure out what that is. If you think it's dangerous, I won't keep any in the house. No matter how pretty Ellen thinks they are."

Travis nodded. He got into the Rambler and set his briefcase flat on the passenger seat and the towel-wrapped sickly green rock on top.

"Pleasure meeting you, sir," he said.

"I'll wait to hear from you," Parnell said.

Travis backed out and drove away.

6

Back at the Cortez Inn, a U-shaped motel where his room was on the left side of the U, Travis sat on the edge of his dark brown bedspread and examined the rock again.

He had gripped it too hard when he first took it out of the towel, and once again little particles flaked off. He gathered them into a tissue so he wouldn't risk losing any more of the specimen.

He thought about how it might have been made.

He wasn't a specialist in minerals, but he knew a few things from his studies. Under certain conditions in nature, sand and rocks could change density and appearance if they were impacted with enough heat.

There was something called fulgurite, or petrified lightning, a kind of primitive glass that was made from lightning hitting sand. Lava rocks were made when molten lava rapidly cooled.

And there were unnatural conditions that could create a kind of glass from sand or rocks. When the Trinity nuclear bomb was tested near Alamogordo, New Mexico in 1945, afterward they found piles of what some people called nuclear glass, or trinitite after the name of the bomb. Some of the rocks were bright green. Alien rocks, some might say. But they were made by man as a by-product of the most destructive new force on earth.

It was that fact which made Travis's heart speed even now.

The heat required to turn brown rocks to green, to give them this malted appearance on the sides—he had seen pictures of the nuclear rocks, and these weren't so different from those.

Nuclear.

Did the visitors possess nuclear weapons?

Were they going to unleash them one day on remote hillsides like this one in scenic Cortez, Colorado?

Were their spaceships powered by nuclear engines?

Was this rock that he held in his hands emitting some kind of radiation or other poison that might kill Travis if he held it too long?

He wished now he hadn't licked it. What a stupid thing to do.

He quickly stowed the rock back inside its towel.

He had two options, that he could see.

Take the rock immediately back to Dr. Linsk and let him examine it for himself. Dr. Linsk had far more experience both as a scientist and as a government advisor. He knew a lot more than Travis did about all of this.

Travis was nobody. Just a post-doc with a wife and baby.

He had ambitions, of course, but not like this. He didn't need to risk his life to get at the truth.

The second option was to stay. Complete the task Dr. Linsk had assigned. Climb back up on the ridge for as many nights as it took to wait for the spaceship to come back, if it ever did.

And thereby expose himself to a nuclear-powered spaceship that might put him at even greater risk.

Travis left the rock wrapped in its towel and underneath his bed, and put on his new thick coat to go take a walk and think.

The afternoon was breezy, but mild. A simply gorgeous day. Golden sun, blue sky, the greens and the yellows of the trees all up and down the street. The smell of something baking at the coffee shop next to the motel.

Travis changed his restless mind.

He got back into the Rambler and drove out in the same direction he did this morning and last night. Out toward the ridge and Parnell's ranch.

Past pastures with horses lazily grazing. Past white-trunked aspens with their bright yellow leaves. Past firs and spruces and cottonwoods. Past civilization, toward the new and unsettling unknown.

Travis glanced often at the ridge to his left. Where a spaceship had lightly touched down, on kitten paws, according to Bart Parnell. Where a certain kind of future awaited Travis and everyone else in the world, whether they were ready for it or not.

But the Rambler drove past the turnoff to the ridge and kept on going another mile or two. Travis found himself parking on a dirt pullout that had access down to the Dolores River.

He shuffled down the gentle embankment in his ordinary leather shoes. He stood at the edge of the water just listening to what the Dolores said.

This was earth. This was Travis's home. In all its beauty, with all its life.

He had a beautiful, happy wife waiting for him ten hours away.

He had a smiling, gurgling baby girl with chubby cheeks and soft chubby arms. He could be holding her ten hours from now.

What was he doing here?

If aliens had really come to such a beautiful, peaceful place, what was Travis supposed to do about that? How could his science protect his wife or child?

He had always been curious, the little boy on his belly watching the ants. The little boy sitting in his back yard for hours, watching the songbirds fill out their days.

But these were different times. A potentially dark and different world.

A world where a president could be shot in broad daylight and no one could stop it. Where nuclear bombs were in the hands of humans.

Where aliens had them, too.

In a dangerous time like this, what difference could Travis really make? He could study pictures of Mars and come up with theories about what was there. He could help Dr. Linsk write his paper for the military about whether they could grow plants in greenhouses built on the moon.

All of it was interesting, the kind of thing Travis the little boy would have loved to do.

But he loved Rosie and baby Caroline more. So much more.

This wasn't the place for him.

He turned away from the clear, tumbling river and climbed back up the incline to his car. He drove back, in a hurry this time, past aspens and evergreens and golden pastures with their grazing horses.

Back into the small town of Cortez where some of its citizens might have alien dirt and alien rocks sitting inside their houses right now.

Things that might poison them and kill them. Travis had a duty to warn them if that was true.

But after that—after that—

He honestly didn't know what he was supposed to do.

He returned to his room at the motel and packed his clothes back into his suitcase. He pulled the alien rock out from under the bed and stowed it in the Rambler's trunk along with his briefcase and his luggage.

He drove to Baxters and returned the coat, the boots, and the gloves. He had all of those back at home. He didn't need to spend the government's money.

He kept the thermal underwear and the wool socks to wear in case it really did snow tonight.

At the little restaurant next door he bought fresh coffee to put in his thermos, and three roast beef sandwiches for the road.

It was late already, but not dark. He could be back in Fort Collins by morning.

A spaceship might land on the ridge tonight, but it would have to land there alone. Travis would not be sitting under a tree waiting for it. Waiting for whatever dangerous thing might happen next. Sacrificing what he had for something unknown.

It was like Rosie said, when she told him she didn't need a fancy wedding. Life was short and love was too important.

Rosie and Caroline were too important by far.

Maybe that was the message of the figurine. Whether it had been crafted by some alien artisan and left here to be found, or randomly molded by the heat of a nuclear-powered spaceship landing or taking off.

Arms open, asking for love.

The symbol of a human life.

Travis already had love. He just had to hurry back home to claim it.

If the end was coming—and he thought now it might —he wasn't going to waste one more minute alone in this world.

THE FACTORY

1

"You need to go underground," Fritz Zimholt said.

Alice didn't realize he meant it literally.

She now followed the retired Air Force Major down a long flight of wide metal stairs into the well-lit cavern below.

Up topside was what presented itself as a private regional airport in the Wasatch Mountain Range of Utah, close enough to the ski resorts surrounding Salt Lake City that a limo ride could get you to any of them within an hour. One of the helicopters could carry an extreme skier to the top of an untracked ridge in even less.

But this airport wasn't for tourists. That became clear as the jet approached a high set of snow-covered peaks. Alice watched with some concern as the jet seemed destined to crash into the mountain.

Instead the peaks disappeared, nothing more than an optical illusion, and suddenly she could see the airport below. The jet met the end of the runway and the pilot, Arnie Camper, brought it to a smooth and polished stop.

The airport's long, red-bricked terminal had cheerful turquoise trim around all the doors and windows, and a forest-green roof that stood out stark against the snowy mountains that rose all around it.

Parked in neat rows in front of the five modestly-sized silver hangars were what appeared to be private jets. They were the kind owned or rented by the rich who could arrive whenever they wanted and bring their Labrador Retrievers with them as they boarded without ever having to take off their shoes or remove metal from their pockets.

Alice had arrived in a jet just like it, along with Major Fritz Zimholt and her friend Marnie Stemple. Both the Major and Marnie were still recovering from their recent injuries: a bullet wound to the Major's shoulder; for Marnie, a concussion, various cuts and deep bruises, and most serious for her, a broken ankle. Marnie was also chronically dehydrated and malnourished, according to the doctor, and though she was near Alice's age, both of them in their late-twenties, Marnie simply wasn't as hardy. She needed rest and recovery.

Marnie fought the doctor on both.

"I'm leaving," she announced just a few days after the shootout that had killed Alice's bodyguard.

Dr. Sabbagh, a stern-looking woman in her mid-forties with olive skin and short black hair, tried her best to dissuade her patient.

"Don't be an idiot," the doctor said. "You're as bad as him." She jerked her chin toward Major Zimholt, who at that moment sat stoically straight-backed on one of the raised hospital beds while a nurse finished changing the dressing on his left shoulder. She then settled his arm back in its padded black sling. The Major struggled to rebutton his shirt one-handed. He relented and allowed the nurse to help.

Marnie didn't seem swayed by the doctor comparing her to the Major. Instead she was even more resolved.

Dr. Sabbagh fitted her with a calf-high orthopedic boot to support her broken ankle and resentfully let her go.

"You make her eat," Dr. Sabbagh warned Alice. "She's not a lab rat, for godssake. She's as human as the rest of you."

Marnie didn't seem to mind the comment, but as the three of them left the infirmary together, Alice felt a smoldering anger. This was the second time Dr. Sabbagh had scolded Alice like that.

Of course Marnie was human. Of course Alice knew it. Had she ever treated Marnie otherwise?

But later, when her anger cooled, Alice wondered about what the doctor said. Why she felt the need to say it.

There were other people, Alice had been told, people like Marnie who had "gifts" of their own.

Maybe Dr. Sabbagh, attending doctor at the Ultra base, had seen some of them before.

Maybe the doctor really did need to remind people from time to time that what they were looking at was human.

With his shoulder injury, Major Zimholt couldn't pilot his jet himself. Although there were other pilots stationed at Ultra, the major insisted on waiting for his own.

Alice felt an unexpected lift when she saw who arrived.

He came trotting down the three steps of the jet and paused in front of the Major to salute. Then he turned to greet the two women.

"Ma'am," Arnie Camper said, giving Alice a friendly two-fingered salute at his temple.

"Alice," she reminded him, extending her hand.

Camper grinned. "Mama taught me it's always best to err on formal. Alice."

His grip was firm, respectful.

He wasn't much taller than she was, maybe five-foot-four, and as weight-conscious as any jockey. He flew the single-seater Stealth Pods—the "Snack Packs"—Alice had first seen about a week ago at the base known as the Aviary.

Camper had been assigned to tailing Marnie on her

twice-daily flights out over the Aviary's open landscape. Alice didn't know if the two had ever actually met.

Alice introduced him and Camper shook Marnie's hand, too. Then Major Zimholt pointed to his own jet a short distance down the airfield, and the four of them set out in that direction.

Alice and Marnie's luggage, a duffel apiece, was already in the cargo hold.

Alice glanced behind her, wondering if Ted Whitling was going to see them off after all. She hadn't talked to him since last night when he briefly joined her for dinner in Cafeteria C, the one closest to the infirmary, and tried once again to talk her out of leaving.

The café-styled cafeteria smelled of Christmas pine, a scent that must have come out of an air freshener. The Ultra base was in New Mexico, on a bare stretch of high desert with no pine trees in sight.

The post-Christmas menu seemed designed to take advantage of some leftovers. Potato pancakes made from mashed potatoes and served with applesauce; turkey sandwiches; and Brussels sprouts sautéed in butter, soft on the inside, crispy on the out. Dessert was cherry pie with ice cream on top. Alice ate half a slice and all of the ice cream.

Ted came in looking tired and slightly harried. In his mid-thirties, solid and fit, he wore shirts that looked tighter than seemed comfortable, but that showed off his muscular arms and chest.

As usual, Alice could see sweat stains in the pits.

Ted ordered a cup of corn chowder and barely ate a bite. As though he, too, had to keep his weight down to pilot a Snack Pack.

"What makes you think you'll be safer with Major Zimholt?" Ted had asked quietly while Alice ate her pie. "I'm not saying you can't trust him, but he doesn't have the kind of security we have here."

Alice gave him a withering look. Four attempts on her life in the past week, two of them at supposedly secure facilities where Ted had brought her to keep her safe.

"I don't have much faith that the Agency can protect me anymore," Alice said. "Major Zimholt took a bullet for me. Right now that wins."

She didn't tell Ted what Major Zimholt said before the gunfire erupted: that he knew Alice's grandfather, Peter Kern, some years ago. That the two of them had worked together somehow, even though Alice's grandfather had been in the Army and Major Zimholt was Air Force.

Most important, he remembered Peter Kern as a good man, a man of loyalty and integrity. That was the grandfather Alice knew, too.

And Major Zimholt knew the name of the man who might have ordered Alice killed.

Alice didn't tell Ted Whitling any of that.

She wasn't sure why. She thought about it as she left

Cafeteria C carrying a bag of takeout containers back to Marnie.

It wasn't that she distrusted Ted Whitling. She didn't. Even though she was no clearer now than she was a week ago when she first met Ted what his exact job was with the government or specifically with the Agency, where Alice worked as an analyst.

She was equally unsure exactly what Major Zimholt's work entailed. Ted had described him as a "consultant." But the facility where he invited both Alice and Marnie to join him wasn't military, Major Zimholt told them, it was owned by his private company.

But it wasn't about putting her faith in one man or the other.

It was that Alice wanted to trust her own instincts more.

And those instincts were telling her to leave this place where once again she had become a ready target.

The offer from Major Zimholt seemed her best choice right now. She didn't know where else she would go.

And so far everything about Major Zimholt made her feel as secure as she could these days, knowing at any moment someone else might try to kill her.

Her instincts told her she could trust him. And she wanted to see where trusting him could lead her.

But even though Alice wasn't doing what Ted Whitling wanted right now, she had a hard time believing he might be off somewhere sulking instead of telling them goodbye. That didn't seem his style.

More likely he was busy receiving or carrying out instructions of some kind. From whom, Alice still didn't know.

"After you," Major Zimholt said, gesturing with his good arm for Alice and Marnie to follow Camper into the jet.

Alice had glanced behind her once more, but her one remaining connection to the Agency had chosen not to see her off.

2

Major Zimholt continued descending the long metal staircase down toward the beckoning lights below. Alice paused on the stairs to look back and check on Marnie.

She was having a slow, laborious time of it, gripping the metal handrail for support while she stepped sideways down each stair first with her good foot, then with the bulky black boot. Good foot, boot.

Alice gave her a look of sympathy.

"Screw it," Marnie muttered.

She bent over and ripped the hook and loop straps free. She pulled off the stiff boot and handed it to Alice.

Then she held her arms out to her sides and launched herself forward, like a diver off the board. She flapped her arms twice, quickly, then glided the rest of the way down.

She landed on her good foot and hopped over to the side where she could lean against the wall.

She looked up at Alice with a smile of satisfaction.

Major Zimholt laughed. "Very good."

He completed his descent, with Alice a few steps behind.

"I didn't think you could take off that way," Alice said.

"I… haven't for a long time," Marnie said, shifting her gaze to the side. She seemed uncomfortable with the question. Alice wasn't sure why.

Normally Marnie had to getting a running start while she flapped her arms hard before she achieved liftoff. Alice had been working with her on a trampoline to see if Marnie could lift up vertically straight from the ground.

This was now a third way, and Alice was glad to see it. She needed Marnie to be safe. The more ways Marnie could get away if she was in danger, the better.

The two of them stood beside Major Zimholt now looking out at the enormous area before them.

It was an underground hangar, as long as the airfield above them and at least three or four times the width. The ceiling stretched above them at least twice the height of the largest hangar back at the Aviary.

The room was well-lit and smelled faintly of damp

concrete. Despite its vast open area, the sound seemed muted, when Alice expected it to echo.

There were workers everywhere. At least fifty, probably more. And they all had plenty to do, tending to the aircraft lined up in rows that stretched all the way to the back.

Alice had never seen aircraft like this. The Snack Packs back at the Aviary were the strangest things she had seen so far. Single-seat jets with round bodies and streamlined wings.

Here there were similarly round craft, but not a wing in sight.

They looked more like spaceships than planes. Or like bubble-shaped submarines someone might use to explore the bottom of the ocean.

"What are they?" Alice asked.

"For now we call them pods," said Major Zimholt. "They're experimental. They won't be ready to share for some time."

One of them at the front of a row suddenly popped upward toward the ceiling like a carbonated bubble rising in a glass. A round opening, the same diameter as the pod, opened in the ceiling, and the craft squeezed through it.

There was no engine noise, no sound associated with it at all.

Another pod moved into position, bubbled up and disappeared.

At the front of a closer row Alice could see Arnie Camper talking to a petite, serious-looking young black woman standing next to a pod. She wore a loose khaki one-piece coverall that made Alice wonder if she was a mechanic.

The young woman suddenly gripped Camper's arm and laughed at something he said.

It shouldn't matter to Alice. She barely knew Camper. They had only talked briefly a few times.

She watched as the woman pulled open her coverall at a center seam and slipped out of the baggy khaki. Underneath she wore a skin-tight gray one-piece that covered her from the neck to where the fabric disappeared into her ankle-high black boots. The outfit looked like a wetsuit.

Alice had seen a suit like that before. It had been waiting in Marnie's drawer for her when they arrived at Ultra a few days ago.

It was so lightweight it puddled in her hand like a silk scarf. Yet its fibers, whatever they were made of, had been strong enough to prevent a bullet from piercing Marnie's chest.

Marnie was looking at the woman now, too.

"Does she fly?" she asked.

"Not like you," said Major Zimholt. "But yes."

The woman pulled the hood of the suit over her head and tucked a few loose strands of her dark hair into its edges like someone wearing a swim cap. Then she reached into the pod beside her and removed what looked like a strip of lights.

She fitted the strip over her head and nestled it against the two bumps that were her ears under the hood.

Last, she removed her boots and stowed them down low inside the pod.

She climbed barefoot into the craft. A round transparent lid closed over her.

A hole appeared in the ceiling above her and she popped straight up and through it.

"Normally you need a security clearance to see what you're seeing now," said Major Zimholt.

"I do have clearance," Alice said.

"Not high enough," the Major said. "But I have some discretion. And these are extenuating circumstances. I believe you two can keep my secrets. As I will keep yours."

There were so many questions Alice wanted to ask, but she couldn't help noticing Marnie's growing agitation.

Her friend was flicking the fingers of her right hand against her left palm. Alice had seen that nervous habit before.

Marnie had been cooped up for the last few hours while the jet brought them from New Mexico to Utah. She needed to fly soon. That short glide down the stairs wasn't enough.

"Is there somewhere Marnie can go?" Alice asked.

Major Zimholt looked at Marnie's clothes. She was wearing thick black leggings and a fleece pullover top. "You'll want to dress more warmly than that," Major Zimholt said. "I had your luggage taken to your rooms. You can change into one of your flight suits—"

"In here is fine," Marnie interrupted. "Is there somewhere out of the way?"

There was a slight bounce to her legs now, as if her body were desperate to run.

But she couldn't run, not with her bad ankle. Alice wasn't sure how she was going to do it.

Major Zimholt pointed to the far right. "There are no flights on that row. Those are all waiting for repairs."

Marnie began hobbling in that direction.

"Can I help?" Alice asked. "I could run along beside you…"

"No need," said Major Zimholt. "I have a better idea."

He removed what looked like an ordinary pen from the zippered chest pocket of his down jacket. He spoke into it.

"Christopher, we need a transfer."

From the space between two rows of pods rose a small craft, smaller than the pods. It hovered at least five feet above the ground and began speeding in their direction.

It had a rounded half-shell in front at waist height,

like a chariot. It came to a stop in front of Major Zimholt and lowered all the way to the ground.

The driver stepped off. He wore a lighted headband like the one Alice had seen on the woman pilot. He began removing it from the crown of his head.

"No, please take Miss Stemple to Row One," said Major Zimholt. To Marnie he said, "We'll teach you how to drive yourself later."

Marnie seemed grateful for no further delay. The driver helped her step onto the back of the chariot. Then the craft rose silently above Alice's head and zoomed Marnie off toward the right.

From the open back of the chariot Alice could see Marnie standing with her feet planted, her hands gripping the waist-high rail in front. The craft came to a stop high above the furthest row of pods.

Marnie leaned over and removed the stiff black boot. She handed it to the driver. Then she turned toward the open lip of the transport, held her arms out to the side, and dove.

She flapped her arms hard several times before shifting into a glide. Then she alternated arms into a swimmer's crawl and moved gracefully through the air.

Alice looked at the workers below her in the well-lit space. A few gazed upward at Marnie. Some even briefly clapped.

Then they went back to whatever their tasks were.

Christopher the chariot driver had already returned his craft to one of the further rows.

"They don't even care," Alice said to the Major. "It's like they see someone flying every day."

"They've seen their share of interesting things," Major Zimholt said. "Marnie will fit right in."

Alice looked up at him, curious.

"What is this place, exactly?"

"It's a factory of sorts," said Major Zimholt. "It's been in my family for decades."

Alice regarded him skeptically. "And if I had the right clearance, what would you say?"

Major Zimholt looked out into the distance and smiled. Alice could see Marnie swimming through the air on her way back toward the front, completing her first full lap.

"Then I could tell you an interesting story," Major Zimholt said. "It's one I think Marnie would like to hear, too.

"But first I'd like you both to meet a scientist friend of mine. She can give you a better sense of what we're dealing with here."

LAS CRUCES 1969

1

Travis Baird parked his white Rambler station wagon at the side of the dusty road. He could see the edge of the pond in the near distance. A man stood on the bank waiting for him.

Benji Moreno looked to be about Travis's age, thirty, with dark brown skin that had seen plenty of sun and a thick black mustache that curved down over the sides of his mouth. He wore faded Levi's, a tan work shirt, dusty cowboy boots, and a straw cowboy hat.

Travis was dressed much the same: worn-in Levi's, a light blue button-down shirt, hiking boots, and a cheap Panama hat that his wife Rosie had picked up for him at a yard sale.

Travis shut the driver's-side door and went around to the back. He kept his kit here, the equipment and tools he had found most useful over the past five years he had been doing this job.

Water retrievals were often tricky. If there wasn't a boat nearby, he sometimes waded or swam, but one site inspection with a Geiger counter had cured him of that. Radiation ten times the normal limit. He wasn't swimming in water like that.

Instead he carefully pulled out the fishing rod that was already rigged with hook and sinkers. He tried not to snag the top of the seat.

A gust kicked up more dust. He coughed. His lungs were getting worse.

"Mr. Baird?" Benji Moreno called.

Travis raised the fishing pole in answer. He understood that Mr. Moreno must be anxious to speak to him, but Travis had learned not to hurry.

The way things were now at his university, he had to do it all by the book. No steps skipped. Nothing that would allow any of his investigations to be discounted, explained away.

He had many masters at the moment. Colorado State University in Fort Collins, Colorado. The U.S. military, two separate branches: Army and Air Force. NASA, when it chose to direct or review his work.

And the Agency, a division of the government that Travis had some ideas about, but no official or complete explanation of who they really were.

He also had an immediate boss, Dr. Alvin Linsk, head

of the Department of Biology at Colorado State University. It was Dr. Linsk who first entrusted Travis with the work that had consumed Travis's life for the last five years.

The work that might, Travis suspected, be killing him.

He slammed shut the back door of the station wagon. The sound carried across the bleak desert landscape. There were no houses out here. Just dirt and creosote bushes and mesquite trees. No traffic. The last car he had seen was at least ten miles back.

Benji Moreno might have a car parked back at his house on the other side of the hill behind him, but he had used different transportation over the rough and challenging land. A brown horse stood grazing on the scrubby grass growing near the pond.

Travis thought he should probably warn Mr. Moreno not to let the horse eat that. But first he would confirm it with his Geiger.

He turned it on and began trudging toward the pond with the Geiger counter in his right hand, fishing pole in his left, resting over his shoulder.

The Geiger counter immediately began chittering at him in the unnerving clicks that sounded like a cross between static and amplified crickets. Travis forced himself to walk slowly, even though the sound always made him want to match the Geiger's pace with his steps.

This was not a job to be hurried. Ever. No matter how nervous each discovery made him.

But why not learn the truth? That was Rosie's question, the first time he came home from a site visit five years ago and told her he was going to quit.

"But if it's real," she said, "don't you think we should know as much as we can?"

They had a new baby daughter, Caroline, just a month old.

"If there's going to be some… invasion," Rosie said. "I want to know ahead of time. We need to protect Caroline."

Now, five years later, there was no doubt in Travis's mind that UFOs were real. Not called UFOs by the faculty—that was for the general, uninformed public. It was the term used in science fiction movies and by the media and by Joe and Jane on the street.

Travis had been trained to call them UAOs: Unconventional Aerial Objects. The distinction was subtle, but scientifically it mattered. Naming things mattered. It often framed people's attitudes.

Calling something an unidentified flying object implied that it might, at some point, *be* identified as some kind of conventional object. That despite what eyewitnesses saw, or what the physical evidence showed, these objects weren't mysterious after all. They were just (take your pick, they had all been claimed) weather balloons or lighthouses or swamp gas or flares. It was the planet Venus. It was kids messing around with flashlights.

Or the witnesses were hallucinating or were liars or were just wrong.

Travis had heard enough and seen enough and done enough lab work by now that he knew who the liars were. They weren't men like Benji Moreno. Travis already knew that just from speaking with Mr. Moreno on the phone.

The Geiger counter chittered ever more enthusiastically the closer Travis got to the pond. Mr. Moreno's horse lifted her head and swiveled her ears toward the frantic sound.

Travis had heard enough. He already knew to be careful. He could take specific readings later.

For now he turned off the Geiger and set it on the dirt. He advanced toward Mr. Moreno, hand outstretched.

"Mr. Moreno," Travis said. "Good afternoon."

"Benji." The man's hand was rough and calloused. Travis always found a kind of honesty in that. He had shaken a lot of soft hands belonging to bureaucrats and professors and even military officers. Give him an honest working man any day.

"That there's Florence," Benji said, pointing to his horse. "You ride, sir?"

"A few times, when I was a kid. And please, it's just

Travis." He watched the mare rip out another mouthful of grass growing on the bank of the pond. "Benji, I don't want Florence to get sick. I'm not sure this grass is safe anymore."

Benji's eyes widened in alarm. "I didn't think of that." He hurried over to the horse and lifted her head by the bridle. He clucked to her softly and patted her dark brown neck. Her heavy black mane fell across her eyes.

Travis had always loved the look of horses. He loved their earthy smell. Now that he was responsible for inspecting reported sites all through the Four Corners area, he got to see horses a lot more often.

The mare now safely in hand, Travis shifted his gaze to the water. He knew from his telephone conversation with Mr. Moreno what to expect, but it was still fascinating to see in person.

A large, flesh-colored disk, about five feet across, floating in the center of the brownish-green water of the pond.

Two nights ago, according to Benji Morales, he and his wife and his brother had all witnessed a group of lights, red and orange and white, hovering above this pond. They could see it over the cap of the hill that separated their property from the county road.

The three of them had scrambled up the hillside on foot until they had a clear view of what was causing the lights.

It was a flat, round metallic-looking aircraft with red and orange lights flickering across its surface. Benji described it as about the size of a helicopter.

A second, smaller craft, this one as round as a baseball, hovered nearby, emitting a bright white light.

"We couldn't see inside," Benji Moreno had said on the phone. "There wasn't any windows."

The two crafts hovered in place for almost half an hour. Neither of them made any sounds. Sometimes the white ball would jerk above the larger craft, stay suspended there a few moments, then jerk back down beneath it.

"I never saw anything like it," Benji told him. "The way it moved. So *fast*."

Travis had heard words almost exactly like that from hundreds of witnesses by now.

Finally without any warning both crafts dashed away at such immediate speed, "We coulda blinked and missed it," Benji said.

Travis had heard reports like that, too. He only wished he could see it for himself, even once. He didn't doubt any of the eyewitness testimony. If anything, it made him long for his own sighting all the more.

He wondered how he would actually feel if he one day—or more likely, night—found himself face to face with one of the spacecraft. Or even more alarming, with one of the aliens.

He had catalogued four different species so far, based on witness descriptions and his own biological assessment of some of the remains that had been shared with Dr. Linsk's lab.

Bodies that were without digestive systems, hearts, and lungs. Without any of the familiar organs Travis would expect to find in any earthly creatures.

What they did have was varying thickness and color of skin and dramatically different skeletal structures, both from humans and from each other.

There were the small Greys, as everyone had started calling them. About three feet tall, with thin gray skin the color of a dolphin. Elongated oval heads that were wider at the top than the chin. Large eyes with double lids, like some sharks. Small, lipless mouths about an inch wide, slits for ears. No reproductive organs or any outward evidence of gender, if there even were male and female distinctions wherever they came from.

Then there were the other three types, with names that seemed specific to the groups talking about them. The tall aliens, some of them six-foot, with scaly skin and large three-fingered hands, were called Reptilites or Lizard People or just RL-40s for no reason Travis had ever been told.

The Whites or the Round-Heads or PR-25s, depending on whether you talked to military or NASA or the Agency, were associated with the cigar-shaped crafts that had been seen flying over Air Force installations in Nevada and New Mexico.

Three of the Whites had been found dead inside a crashed spaceship near Socorro, New Mexico. They were slightly larger than the Greys, maybe four-foot at most, with pale round faces, round black eyes with just a single layer of eyelids, and wider mouths than the Greys, about three inches across.

Last were the Clones. Although Travis preferred to call them by their alpha-numerical name, AR-10s. These aliens, more than any of the others, gave Travis actual nightmares.

Not because they were so different from us. Because they were the *same*.

He had never told Rosie about them. It was one of the few secrets he kept from her. The implications were too grave. He couldn't bear to think about them himself.

The first time Dr. Linsk brought Travis into the lab to show him an entire arm someone had salvaged, Travis thought he was looking at the victim of a car accident.

The skin tone, the bone structure, even the musculature and circulatory system, looked exactly like a human's. There were little human-looking hairs all along the forearm.

"This is new," Dr. Linsk told him. His own face looked unusually pale. "Got it from Wright-Patterson."

Travis knew the place, of course. Wright-Patterson Air Force Base in Ohio had become a kind of clearinghouse for whatever was found at crash sites—whether spaceships or bodies.

"I-I don't understand," Travis said.

Dr. Linsk pointed at the arm. "That's not human. I've seen a picture of the whole body. Damn thing could be you or me."

Dr. Linsk swiped the back of his hand over his mouth. Travis could see sweat on his boss's cheeks.

"I want you to take that thing apart," he told Travis. "Tell me what every microscopic speck of it is made of. We're the ones who're going to tell Washington how to tell if someone who looks like Nixon really is Nixon."

"You're joking," Travis said. Sweat was blanketing his own face now.

"I need a drink," Dr. Linsk said. He left to go get one.

It didn't take Travis long to make his first discovery.

He tracked down Dr. Linsk at the bar where the two of them sometimes went. Travis sat next to him and ordered a whiskey. He drank it in two gulps.

"There are no cells," he whispered to Dr. Linsk.

"No..." He rested his forehead against his hand.

Travis sat holding his empty glass, staring straight ahead.

Dr. Linsk reached over and gripped his arm.

"Well, thank God for that," Dr. Linsk said, rising from his stool. He paid for his drink and walked out of the bar.

Travis caught up with him out on the sidewalk that led back to campus. The day was warm, but the walkway was shady beneath the green ash trees and American elm.

"It's a good start," Dr. Linsk said as he strode quickly back toward the lab. "But they're going to want a hundred different things. Two hundred, if you can find them. Some way of knowing at a glance whether the guy you're talking to is who you're supposed to be talking to."

"And Travis," he said, coming to an abrupt halt. The sunlight through the trees made it look like a golden halo glowed behind his head. "This thing is the goddamned worst thing we've ever seen." He looked around and lowered his voice. "I don't care if those Godzilla lizard-people start crashing into supermarkets tomorrow. At least we know what we're in for. Army'll take them out in a heartbeat.

"But this." He blew out a bourbon-scented breath. "Damn. Won't know who to trust. You see that, don't you?"

"Yes, sir," Travis said. He could feel the coldness of that truth freezing the chambers of his speeding heart.

"Give me *something*," Dr. Linsk said. "Maybe whoever has the head can say there's something about their eyes. But we're the arm men, Travis. You tell me about that arm."

Travis had labored long and fearfully to gather as much information from the arm as he could.

His report, nearly a hundred pages with appendices, photos, and lab results, went off to whichever master had sent them the arm in the first place. Travis didn't know which one it was. Military, NASA, Agency.

But he kept a copy for himself. Something he was strictly forbidden to do.

He kept it because he already knew by then that he might not live long enough to protect Rosie and Caroline if the worst should ever happen.

"You need my help?" Benji Moreno asked. He still stood beside Florence, stroking her long brown neck and keeping a tight hold on her bridle.

"I'll let you know," Travis said.

He had gotten fairly good at casting, even though he had still never fished for pleasure. It wasn't one of the skills his father taught him.

But enough water retrievals had honed his aim. He hit the flesh-colored disk in the center of the pond on his first try.

He began reeling it in.

"What do you think it is?" Benji asked.

"Could be a bubble of spent fuel," Travis said, knowing it wasn't that at all. He wasn't supposed to discuss much of the science with members of the public.

As he pulled the disk the last few feet onto shore, he heard snorting and a whinny behind him.

Florence's eyes were wide. Travis could see white all around her brown pupils. She jerked back on the bridle, trying to drag Benji and herself away.

"I'd take her over there," Travis said, gesturing toward the distant hill. He'd been around horses and dogs at various sites, but this was the first time he'd seen an animal react this way.

He let the fishing line go slack so he could see which way the wind blew it. It was coming toward him, which also meant toward where Florence had been standing. Was there a smell? Travis couldn't detect it himself. Just the usual odor of rotting vegetation around any kind of pond.

He went back for his Geiger counter and turned it on again.

The clicks accelerated even before he held the instrument directly over the flesh-colored disk.

Once he did, the machine lost its mind.

He quickly turned it off.

And once again had a decision to make.

How much exposure could he continue to survive?

The radiation was consuming his body.

He wasn't the only scientist with deep, hacking coughs that never improved. With skin lesions and muscle soreness and a host of other symptoms.

Sometimes they talked to each other about it, in alcohol-fueled whispers.

"Heard Dave Thompson died last week."

"How old?"

"Thirty-eight."

"Shit."

"What about Gene Whittacker last month? Lung cancer."

"How old?"

"Forty-two."

It was the question they all wanted to know: *How old?*

Meaning, *How much more time do I have?*

The boys in the field weren't lasting very long. The ones in the labs had better armor. Lead-lined bibs and protective helmets and gloves.

But the people in charge didn't want to spook the public.

Travis couldn't show up in a fully shielding suit while unsuspecting citizens played with alien artifacts and biological remnants with their bare hands. While Benji Moreno and his mare breathed in through their noses and lungs whatever alien fumes might be emitted.

"I'll be back in a minute," Travis told Benji. "Please don't touch this. I need to make sure it's safe."

Benji nodded, but Travis could see his burning curiosity. He would have felt the same way.

"I don't mind you looking at it," he added, since Benji would do that in any case. "But make sure you keep Florence away from it."

There was little danger of her coming closer. The mare backed away from the thing on the bank of the pond every chance that Benji gave her.

Travis hiked back to the Rambler. From the resistance he'd felt on the fishing line, he knew the flesh-colored disk was heavy. He would need his sturdiest container.

It would be easier to transport the disk in pieces, but he didn't want to cut it open out here in the field. He had made that mistake once before with what looked like a solid organism, black as coal, that he tried to cut open just at the edge.

The thing bled so much black inky liquid, Travis wondered if he had cut open an artery in the organism by accident. He had to staunch the inky flow with first the shirt off his back, then all of the extra clothes packed in his luggage. Ever since then he carried a whole stack of old towels that Rosie had generously donated to the effort.

The Air Force had donated something more useful for right now: a collapsible metal box that Travis could adjust to size. He grabbed a set of metal tongs, too. He didn't want to have to handle this thing.

A scream erupted behind him.

Travis spun around toward the pond.

He dropped the tongs and took off running. Benji Moreno was writhing on the ground.

Dust rose in the distance where the horse was

galloping away. Back toward the hill where Benji Moreno's house lay safely tucked on the opposite side.

Travis's heart hammered in his chest. He raced to the pond at full speed.

The scientist in him took apart everything his eyes took in:

The flesh-colored blob, now a darker brown.

Benji Moreno within reach of it.

The shape of the fleshy disk, contorting into humps and waves, no longer flat.

Benji Moreno screaming. Like the disk was burning him alive.

The sight of Benji's outstretched arm, the fingers blackened, the hand destroyed.

Travis ripped his shirt off. He was nearly there, just a few feet away.

He dragged Benji backward across the dirt and then wrapped Benji's burning hand inside his shirt.

Benji still screamed. His eyes were as wide as Florence's had been.

"What did you do?" Travis shouted over the screams. "Tell me!"

But Benji was past words. All he could do was shriek.

Travis looked back at the thing on the bank. It was growing now, rising from the mud.

The flesh was the same sun-darkened color as Benji Moreno.

Travis thought he could see two legs starting to form.

He didn't want to touch it, My God, not touch it, but he couldn't just stand by and let it build.

He saw the Geiger counter nearby, and scooped it up on a run.

He swung it hard against the creature. It fell backward toward the water.

Benji was crying, yelling, in terrible pain.

"Help me!" Travis shouted. The disk was reforming, rising again.

He swung the Geiger at the top of the shape, at what might be trying to become a head. It jerked back, but it seemed to recover.

There was an arm now. An arm and a hand.

"Benji! Come on!"

The screaming had stopped. The pain was gone.

Travis looked around for any kind of weapon he might use.

Benji Moreno was dead on the ground.

Travis kicked at the mutating disk with his sturdy hiking boots. Kicked and kicked and kicked.

He didn't want to touch it with his bare hands. His gloves were back in the car.

He lifted his knee and aimed the sole of his boot and sent the creature flying backward into the pond.

Travis sped back toward the Rambler, his arms pumping hard, his boots pounding harder. His breath was a piston engine. His lungs felt clogged with tumors and fear.

He risked looking back, to see if it followed, but it was still in the pond as far as he could tell. Whatever it was it had killed Benji Moreno, and Travis still didn't understand how.

He slammed the rear door of the station wagon closed and raced around to the side. His fingers weren't working. He fumbled with the keys. His hands were shaking too hard to meet the ignition.

He let loose a scream of his own just to bleed away some of his fear. He took a deep breath, even though there was no time for that, and he managed to get the keys in and start the car.

He turned the wheel and jammed the gas and the Rambler skidded at first in the dirt. But Travis righted it and drove away from that place and kept driving and driving for miles.

Stress flooded his veins. He could feel it plunging into his heart and out. His breath came out in gasps. He had to slow down, he was going to black out.

He pulled over at the side of the road. The sun glared down at him, too bright to bear.

Travis got out and walked around to the passenger's side and bent over and puked in the dust.

His lungs heaved, desperate for air.

His fists were clenching with some automatic reaction.

Breathe, breathe.

The sight of Benji's blackened hand was still burned behind his eyes.

Was that one of them? One of the clone aliens? Is that how they did it? A spaceship left one of the organisms behind, and some human couldn't resist touching it?

Then the organism took on the physical features. Skin color. All the rest.

Was that arm Dr. Linsk had inside the lab from one of the spaceship crashes—or from something like this?

Had some other unsuspecting witness been killed and duplicated, and someone else had destroyed it before it got too far?

Was there a secret report lying in someone's safe right now, warning the masters about what might happen to their scientists in the field?

Travis wiped his hand across his mouth. He was sick at heart. Sick in the head.

It was too much now. Too much. He wasn't made for this. Maybe someone else was.

He had a five-year-old daughter whose life was precious to him. He had a wife that he loved so much he sometimes wondered how he ever lived before he met her.

He knew enough now. Enough. He could tell Rosie the truth. He already had.

The UAOs were real. Aliens were real. Travis had studied three different species himself.

Four. Four now. He would tell her the truth. She needed to know. To protect their daughter.

How old?

Travis was thirty. Would he live to see thirty-one?

Benji Moreno didn't.

Travis's legs shook as he stumbled back into the Rambler. He closed the door and sat motionless behind the wheel.

Steps. There were steps to take now. People to contact. Calls to make.

Not the local sheriff. No local authorities of any kind. This was a matter only for his bosses.

He would call Dr. Linsk first. Tell him there had been an incident.

Let Dr. Linsk make the other calls. But Travis would have to stay nearby in his motel room in Las Cruces and wait for other investigators to come. He would have to take them out there. Show them.

And what, exactly, would all of them see?

Would Benji Moreno's body still be recognizable, or would the whole thing be blackened down to his bones?

Would the flesh-colored disk, now Benji-colored, still be there where Travis kicked it, or would it have escaped before anyone could find it?

Travis felt bile rising up in his throat again. He swallowed hard to keep it down.

He gripped the steering wheel with his left hand and turned the key with his right.

The sooner he found a phone, the sooner this night-mare could continue.

Travis drove down the dusty road, every beat of his heart begging him to live.

THE LAB

Caroline Baird leaned against the stainless steel counter of her small, custom-built lab and ate her first meal of the day.

A snack baggie filled with plain almonds.

A cup of very welcome coffee.

She needed to stop working sometimes. Let the ideas stop swirling in her head.

But it was hard to stop. There was still so much left to do.

She was fifty-five, with shoulder-length wavy gray hair and cloudy brown eyes that seemed to be getting worse every month.

The lenses in her glasses were so thick now, they required special frames.

The yellow particle microbeam couldn't help her eyesight. She knew that. It would blind her completely.

But the urge was always there to just try.

Instead, she adapted. This lab was part of it. Just eight hundred square feet, filled with two long stainless steel counters, both with sinks, and a freezer where she kept some of the samples.

Two large white boards took up one of the walls so that Caroline could make notes in her own large handwriting and be able to see them at a glance.

In the corner, a desk held her computer and two large display screens. She had been sitting there all morning, reviewing some of the latest findings out of the Red Zone group, then comparing them with information in the database she created out of reports written over fifty years ago.

Finally her eyes began to blur. No point fighting it. She had to stop and allow them to rest, no matter how anxious she was to keep going.

Caroline popped another handful of almonds in her mouth. She set down the baggie and wrapped both hands around her hot mug. She closed her eyes and breathed in the dark rich steam from the coffee, then took another long drink.

What did he mean?

How many times a day did she ask herself that? Poring over her father's notes, all of them transcribed into her database. Studying his drawings and descriptions of every artifact he ever found. Recalling every conversation she had with him.

Travis Baird held the key to so many of the mysteries his daughter Caroline felt so desperate to unlock.

But Travis Baird couldn't help her anymore.

She had to stop wishing for the answers to come from someplace else.

She had to find them inside her own overloaded mind.

The door to the lab opened. Caroline normally worked alone in this quiet and isolated place—she insisted on it, to eliminate any possible distractions—but this was a familiar and welcome face.

Fritz Zimholt, Caroline's current employer and chief supporter for many years before that.

Her brief smile fell.

Why was Fritz's arm in a sling?

"What happened?" she asked, alarmed.

Fritz was the closest she had to a father now. Even in his seventies, he still always seemed indestructible.

She was counting on that.

"Nothing of consequence," he said as he ushered in two women Caroline didn't know.

She squinted to make them out.

The taller one was pale and thin, with short brown hair cut in a pageboy. The shorter woman had dark brown skin and thick brown hair she wore in a long ponytail.

As they came closer, Caroline could see that the taller one walked with a limp.

"This is Dr. Caroline Baird," Fritz told the two women. "She's our chief scientist. Caroline, this is Marnie Stemple and Alice Kern."

Caroline's face went slack.

"Kern?" she repeated.

Fritz shot her a warning look.

Caroline turned quickly away, pretended to fuss over her bag of almonds and the cup of coffee.

Kern.

She would have to ask Fritz about that later.

But from the look he gave her, Caroline already knew she must be right.

Alice Kern bore some relation to Will Kern. Maybe she was even his daughter. The age looked about right.

If so, it was no accident she had found her way to the Factory at last.

When Caroline turned around again, she made sure not to stare at Alice. Instead, she glanced down at the stiff black boot around Marnie's lower leg.

"What happened there?" Caroline asked.

"Broken," Marnie answered. "Major Zimholt said... you might be able to help?"

"I can," Caroline said. "But first let's see to that arm. What happened?" she asked Fritz again.

"A stray bullet," he said. "It can wait."

"But I won't," Caroline said, already reaching to undo the sling.

When Fritz seemed ready to protest, Caroline said, "Let her see it on you first."

Fritz relented.

He removed the sling himself. Caroline helped him peel away his puffy down-filled coat and unzipped the top of his sweater so she could see underneath.

She removed the bandage at the front of his shoulder and exposed the wound.

"That must have hurt like hell," she said, trying to sound nonchalant. But the truth was, seeing the ugly, gaping red circle in his papery skin made her heart beat too fast.

He was old. She knew that. But she needed him to live for a long, long time.

What Caroline wanted and what might happen were two separate matters.

She knew that.

But in this one thing, she preferred to ignore the rules of human science.

At least until she could modify them with the research she was doing.

Caroline left Fritz and the two women momentarily while she gathered her supplies from the locked metal cabinet at the back of the lab. It opened at the imprint of her palm—and only hers.

It wasn't that she didn't trust her colleagues.

The tools within the cabinet were dangerous. She knew that better than anyone else.

And the temptation to use them…

She knew that, too.

Caroline returned with a small black leaded blanket the size of a hand towel, and with what looked like a crude, oversized pistol. It was made of dull gray metal bent in half at a ninety-degree angle, and was a little too large to be comfortable in her hand.

But it was incredibly lightweight. She couldn't believe it the first time she picked it up.

She set the two items on the stainless steel counter.

She made one more trip to the cabinet and brought back eye protection: a welder's helmet for her, fitted with a specially modified auto-darkening filter, and special glasses for Fritz and the two women that wrapped all the way around the sides of their eyes.

Caroline slipped the helmet over her head and waited for the others to don their glasses.

She draped the leaded blanket over Fritz's shoulder. She checked the location of the wound once more, then placed her finger over the spot on top of the blanket.

She picked up the oversized pistol.

It had no exterior hardware. No trigger or hammer. It responded to bare touch.

Caroline slid the barrel of the pistol under the blanket and held it directly against where she knew the wound to be.

Then she shifted her right thumb to where the metal bent, where the hammer would be if it really were a revolver.

At the touch of her skin, the pistol hummed.

Neon green light flared from beneath the leaded blanket.

She didn't need to see it to know what was happening underneath. A particle microbeam shot from the pistol into Fritz's shoulder. In the center of the neon green stream was a thin thread of bright yellow that pulsed like pellets of light into Fritz's wound.

Caroline counted to four.

She removed her thumb from the pistol and slipped the barrel out from underneath the blanket.

She pulled off her welder's helmet and leaned close to examine Fritz's skin.

The wound was completely gone.

Marnie and Alice removed their glasses and stared at Fritz's shoulder with looks of amazement, but not, Caroline was satisfied to notice, fear.

"No side effects, that we're aware of," Caroline told Marnie.

Although that wasn't strictly true.

"Would you like me to fix your ankle?"

Marnie had already leaned over and was undoing the straps across her boot.

"What is it?" Alice asked.

Caroline exchanged a look with Fritz.

"The short version," Fritz told her.

"Are you sure?" Caroline asked. They didn't normally share their secrets with outsiders.

Caroline didn't know these two women. They could be anybody.

Even Alice Kern.

But Caroline trusted Fritz, and when he nodded, she did as he asked.

"It's something my father found," Caroline said. "Something… given to him. By an alien."

THE PACKAGE

1

Marnie and Alice followed Major Zimholt in silence through the warren of interconnecting corridors that led away from Caroline Baird's lab.

Energy hummed through Marnie's veins, like the hum of the device that had completely healed her wounded ankle.

She felt... joy. That was the only word she could call it. Joy at something so mysterious and new.

Alien.

Was it possible?

So many things were possible. Marnie should know that better than anyone.

She glanced aside at Alice, whose face showed no joy whatsoever.

She looked grim. Or maybe just worried.

Marnie bumped her arm against Alice's to try to shake her out of it. "It's fine," Marnie said. "It's good."

"Major Zimholt," Alice said, coming to a stop in the middle of a long corridor. A man in khaki Carhartt pants and a dark green fleece jacket walked by, going in the opposite direction. He nodded to Major Zimholt, but didn't stop.

"What is this place?" Alice asked, looking up at Major Zimholt and keeping her voice low. "What exactly do you do here?"

Marnie could hear the suspicion in Alice's voice. As though she felt tricked, somehow, in coming here.

Marnie didn't understand her attitude. So far this place had exceeded Marnie's own expectations.

To be healed with the blast of an alien device, when Dr. Sabbagh had said it would take weeks for Marnie's ankle to recover.

What other miraculous secrets did Major Zimholt's factory hold?

"I said I would tell you the story," Major Zimholt answered Alice, "and I will. Let me show you to your rooms first."

They made two more turns, one left, one right, past a decent-sized kitchen, what looked like a well-equipped gym, and past rows of closed and numbered doors. Finally Major Zimholt came to a halt in front of two identical doors, marked 23 and 24.

Both doors bore bluish-white squares of fiberglass or

some other transparent material in the center, large enough for a handprint.

"This wing houses the guest quarters," said Major Zimholt. "I hope you will find them comfortable."

"Are there other guests?" Alice asked.

"A few overnights, like Captain Camper," said Major Zimholt. "He does double duty as a test flight pilot here and at the Aviary. I presume he'll return there tomorrow."

"So… the military knows about this place?" Alice asked.

"Oh, yes," said Major Zimholt. "We're one of their contractors."

He laid his right palm flat against the bluish-white panel on door 23. A light passed over his palm. "Now you," he said to Alice.

She repeated the step and the panel emitted a beep. "It will now open for only you," said Major Zimholt. He moved to the door to their right. "Now Marnie, your turn."

He activated the lock with his palm and Marnie added her own. Then she placed her hand on the panel again and the door to room 24 opened inward.

Someone had already brought her duffel to the room. It sat on a neatly-made queen-sized bed with a navy blue bedspread on top. Next to the bed was an oak nightstand with a lamp and digital clock that didn't appear to be plugged in at the moment.

A dark red upholstered chair sat next to another small table in the opposite corner. A floor lamp lit the area.

Beyond the small bedroom, Marnie could see the open door leading to a bathroom.

Unlike the suite at the Ultra military base, this room didn't have a microwave or small fridge or even a coffee maker. It was as small as the room she stayed in at the Aviary base, but nicer looking. Cozier.

Alice had opened her own door and briefly examined the room.

"Where shall we talk?" she asked Major Zimholt.

Marnie could still hear tension in her voice.

"My room is fine," Marnie offered. Close quarters, but she was as anxious as Alice to hear whatever Major Zimholt would tell them about this facility embedded deep inside a mountain.

Marnie stepped inside and claimed a spot at the head of her bed. Alice sat at the foot of it, facing Major Zimholt as he settled into the dark red chair.

"How do I know we're safe here?" Alice asked.

"We have far more security than at either of the bases where you've been," said Major Zimholt. "But I'll be happy to take you on a tour and show you the measures we've taken."

Alice nodded. "Later."

She shot a look at Marnie that Marnie wasn't sure

how to interpret. Alice looked wary. Her body taut. Lines creased her forehead.

Whereas Marnie felt more relaxed now that she did even at the Aviary, when she could fly as much as she wanted and never felt the restless edginess that had dominated her life for the past eleven years.

And even if Alice didn't wholly trust Major Zimholt, Marnie did.

It was more than mere trust.

There was something about the tall, dignified Major that made her feel calm, protected. Safe in a way she hadn't felt safe for many years.

She had been without any family since her mother died when she was seventeen. Marnie never knew her father.

Her mother's parents were both gone by the time Marnie was little. If they ever held her, she couldn't remember.

So she allowed herself this secret wish, something she would never tell anyone else. That Major Zimholt was her long-lost grandfather. That he had returned to take care of her.

Marnie knew it was ridiculous. Of course none of it was real. It was like having a hopeless crush on a celebrity.

Yet the more she watched Major Zimholt, the more time she spent around him, she couldn't help believing her wish was true.

She admired the way he carried himself, the way he spoke to people, the calm way he dealt with his injury. The way he had protected Alice back at Ultra as soon as he saw she was in danger.

It wasn't his fault that Marnie fell into the path of his first bullet. If she knew him better then, she might never have interfered. She could have assumed the Major had everything under control. She was close to believing it now.

Calling for that transport back in the hangar, making sure Marnie could fly even with her injured ankle. She didn't have to explain herself or ask.

Then taking her to Dr. Baird so she could be healed.

Alice was the same way, understanding what Marnie wanted and needed, even without her asking.

Between the two of them, Marnie was starting to feel safe for the first time since she was a teenager.

"What did Dr. Baird mean about an alien giving that tool to her father?" Alice asked. "Alien, as in extraterrestrial?"

"Do you not believe they exist?" Major Zimholt asked.

Alice hesitated before answering.

"I mean… I assume we're not alone in this universe," she said. "It would be arrogant to think otherwise. But the idea that one of them would come here and hand over alien technology to humans…"

"Do you have any more of it?" Marnie asked.

Major Zimholt's eyes seemed to light up. "Oh, yes," he told her. "This entire facility exists because of it."

There it was again, that thrill of joy rushing through Marnie's veins.

Why? Why did it make her so happy to hear?

Because it means I'm not alone.

Ever since that night in the Alaskan wilderness, under the lights of the Aurora Borealis, Marnie had felt alone. Alone in her freakishness. Her bizarre and uncontrollable compulsion.

Alone and isolated, even from her mother. Even though she should have felt closer to her mother than anyone. Just the two of them, sharing this secret.

But it already began driving them apart from the moment Marnie took flight off the surface of the snow.

But if there were aliens—actual, verifiable aliens. Not some fantasy, but utterly real.

And if Major Zimholt, this stalwart, dignified man, believed in their existence—

Maybe, if he even had *proof*—

Then it meant Marnie wasn't the worst of it.

She wasn't the most bizarre.

She wasn't the only anomaly, the singular specimen set apart from the human race.

So yes, it gave her a strange comfort to hear.

Too strange to try to explain to anyone else, even Alice, who knew the truth about Marnie's condition.

"The history of this facility begins some years back," said Major Zimholt.

Marnie scooted against the headboard of her bed and gripped one of the pillows in her arms.

Like this was story time. Like she was a child again.

So ridiculous, yet something she couldn't deny wanting, just for this brief time, in this small, unfamiliar room, with these two people she hoped she could trust.

Marnie knew that real life would return soon enough.

She hadn't forgotten for even a moment what she overheard Alice's former bodyguard, Santos, say to someone giving him instructions through his hidden earpiece.

"Should I grab her now or still wait?"

Someone wanted Marnie captured.

Who, and for what purpose, she didn't know.

But for now, Marnie allowed herself to be happy.

Even if happiness and safety were both just fantasies left over from the childhood she used to have.

2

"My parents and I emigrated from Germany in 1951," Major Zimholt began. "I was six years old. My father had been an unwilling soldier in the German army. He hated Hitler and everything he stood for. But the men of our country had no choice.

"My father was a math tutor before the war. One of his professors knew mathematicians and scientists who emigrated to the U.S. before we did. One of them you might have heard of: Wernher von Braun."

"I do know that name," Alice said. "But I don't know why."

"Initially he worked for Hitler," said Major Zimholt. "Von Braun was a genius, no question. He developed the Nazis' most successful rocket. But then Hitler lost the war, and von Braun surrendered to the Americans. He turned his talents to our space program and became a director for NASA. He was one of the reasons we could get to the moon."

"And your father worked for him?" Marnie asked.

"For people von Braun knew in California. Then a few years later, in 1961, von Braun called my father. He said he needed to show him something."

Major Zimholt paused and took something out of the pocket of his dark wool trousers. He leaned forward and handed it to Alice, who was closest.

It was a small swatch of gray fabric, about half the size of Alice's phone. She picked it up and felt it between her fingers. It was soft, but also seemed strong.

She handed it to Marnie.

"It's like my flight suit," Marnie said.

"Very much," said Major Zimholt. "This was where my father first had the idea. I've made some modifications over time, but the original construction was my father's."

"What's it made of?" Alice asked.

She could hear the tremor in her voice. She bit her teeth together. She could feel them begin to shake.

She couldn't say why she felt frightened now. She had faced far worse than hearing that extraterrestrials might be real.

But right now she would have preferred a more tangible, knowable danger, than this one that challenged the very foundations of what she felt was real.

It was the same as when she first saw Marnie flying.

It made her question her grip on reality.

It made her question her own sanity.

"Tell me what you think of it first," Major Zimholt said to Marnie, motioning toward the swatch of fabric.

Marnie slid it between her thumb and forefinger. "Like silk," she said, "but stronger."

"Stretch it," said Major Zimholt.

Marnie clasped it in both hands and pulled it apart. The fabric lengthened for a moment, then when she let go it snapped right back.

"You can't cut it or rip it or burn it," said Major Zimholt. "It's not like anything we have on Earth."

He paused and looked from Marnie to Alice.

"Is that the point?" Alice asked, her pulse quickening. "It's not from Earth?"

"There was a crash in the desert of New Mexico in 1947," said Major Zimholt. "Perhaps you've heard of it. A place called Roswell."

Alice involuntarily scoffed. "I'm sorry," she told Major Zimholt, who was obviously being sincere. "But everyone knows that's a hoax."

"They do, yes," Major Zimholt agreed. "Just like the idea of a woman who can fly must be a hoax."

"It's not the same thing," Alice said. Although she knew the argument was weak.

Hadn't she been thinking much the same only a moment ago?

"Only because you've seen Marnie do it with your own eyes, and so you know it's true. I understand," said Major Zimholt, holding up his hand to ward off any more objections. "My father felt the same way. He had great respect for Professor von Braun, but clearly the man was disturbed."

"But your father must have changed his mind," Marnie said.

"He did," said Major Zimholt. "He was working at a lab with physicists and chemists who were already doing top secret projects for the government. My father brought the fabric to them and asked them to test it. They couldn't identify a single element of it. They all agreed, as incredible as it sounded, that the fabric was not from our world."

Major Zimholt was undoubtedly a rational man. Still, Alice held on to hope that he was wrong. That he had been fooled, as so many other people must have been fooled over the years, by the manufactured proof that UFOs and aliens were among us.

"Can I see it again?" she asked Marnie.

Alice's hands trembled as she took possession of the swatch. She studied it more closely. It had long thin fibers running in a single direction. As she stared at it under the light from the nearby lamp, there were moments when the fiber seemed metallic.

"Stretch it widthwise," said Major Zimholt. "Watch closely."

Alice gripped the swatch on its sides and stretched as hard as she could.

The fibers, which a second ago had run vertically, readjusted in her hands to stretch horizontally with Alice's pull.

"Whoa." She dropped the gray swatch on the blue bedspread.

Marnie picked it up and repeated the experiment, pulling in the opposite direction of the new grain. The fibers shifted once again to run horizontally with her pull.

Marnie grinned and set the fabric on the bedspread between her and Alice.

"Von Braun was part of an elite group of scientists and military intelligence officers who had been tasked with a top secret mission," said Major Zimholt. "To take artifacts from the Roswell crash and split them among various military contractors and scientific consultants they felt that they could trust. Von Braun trusted my father."

"What was he supposed to do?" Marnie asked.

"What all of them were," said Major Zimholt. "Try to reverse-engineer the items that were found at the crash. Weapons, communication devices, power sources, the design of the spacecraft, all of it."

"But we would have heard about it," Alice objected. "If somebody was making weapons or—or fabric that came out of some alien technology…"

"That was part of the agreement," said Major Zimholt. "No one should ever know. If anyone were able to make these things, they should take credit for it themselves. File for the patents, make the money from it, everything."

"Why?" Marnie asked.

"They didn't want the public to panic," said Major Zimholt. "Think of how ordinary people would react if they knew aliens were spying on our military facilities, and that one had accidentally crashed nearby.

"No, all that von Braun and the others wanted was to discover how to copy the technology for ourselves. Then we could use it against other countries if they tried to attack us, or even against aliens who might wish us harm."

Alice got up from the bed. She needed to move. This was all too crazy. And Major Zimholt was talking about it as if it was normal.

What would her mother say? She was a medical doctor. Would she believe any of this? What about her father, always the skeptic? What would he think about Major Zimholt's story?

Alice admired her parents' calm and rational way of thinking. She tried to apply it in her own work as an analyst with the Agency.

She drew upon those skills now.

"What proof is there?" she asked. "I'm sorry, Major Zimholt, I don't mean to be disrespectful—"

"But it sounds outlandish," he said. "I know. There is

very little written proof. I'm certain you can understand why. Discussions were usually held in person. But even the few memos someone might find in archives in Washington, D.C. only refer to what we were told to call 'the Package.' Nothing more.

"But there is physical proof," he went on. "It still exists, just like that piece of fabric my father brought home when I was sixteen. There are other artifacts from the crash still in people's possession all over the country. I only know about some of them. I suspect there are many."

"Were they able to reverse-engineer all of them?" Marnie asked. Alice noticed she seemed far more accepting of the story. Excited to hear more.

"Not all of them," said Major Zimholt, "but more than you might expect."

"And what are these things?" Alice asked, trying to tamp down the cynicism in her voice. "Would we have heard of any of them?"

Major Zimholt began counting them out on his fingers. "Lasers, night-vision goggles, fiber optics, microprocessors, silicone chips, the material in Kevlar vests... to name a few."

Alice blinked a few times, stunned by the list. Again, it seemed too incredible.

"And if I researched those," she said.

"Their history would be well known," said Major Zimholt. "Invented by this person on this date, patent number, et cetera. Some of the products, like night-vision goggles, were already in the process of being designed. Hitler had a rudimentary version of them himself. But the alien version was far superior. Receiving the Package helped accelerate the process."

Major Zimholt leaned back in the red upholstered chair, relaxed as though awaiting further questions.

Alice remained standing, too agitated to sit down. She reached onto the bed and picked up the swatch of mysterious gray cloth.

"This was found at Roswell," she said, holding it up.

"Yes," said Major Zimholt.

She tried once again to tug it apart. It was strong, but a lot of fabrics were strong. It didn't mean they came from outer space.

Major Zimholt met Alice's troubled gaze. "But you still don't believe me."

"I'm sorry," Alice said. "I don't."

She sat on the edge of the bed again, too tired at the moment to continue questioning him.

"I believe you," Marnie said. "I believe all of it. I know there are things beyond our normal world."

She pointed at herself.

Alice smiled briefly in response. Then her face grew somber again.

"It's all science fiction," she said. "It sounds like it anyway. I'd love to believe it, too. But there are so many other things I need to worry about right now. Alien technology is pretty low on the list."

"What about Dr. Baird's device?" Marnie asked her. "You saw for yourself. It healed my ankle. It healed Major Zimholt's shoulder."

Alice couldn't deny that. She would be a fool to even try. But it gave her a hard pit in her stomach. She clutched at her belly now, just to give herself some comfort.

Major Zimholt must have understood. It was too much. Alice needed to process it all. "We've talked enough for now," he said. "An old man needs his rest."

Alice scoffed. This man was far from old.

But she wasn't sorry to end the conversation. She felt a hundred years old herself.

Major Zimholt rose from the dark red chair and moved to the door. He paused there and turned back to them.

"I do understand," he told Alice. "When my father came home that night and told us everything von Braun said, my mother was just like you. She was a practical German woman. She didn't believe in fairy tales.

"But the time came when she believed without any doubt. I think I can convince you, too."

Alice closed her eyes and pinched her fingers against the edges. Her heart banged inside her chest.

Why am I so afraid?

Not afraid, maybe, but... unwilling. Defiant and unwilling to believe.

She had put aside all of this—fantasy, imagination, belief in the magical and supernatural—six years ago, after her parents were murdered.

For months afterward she still held out some hope of seeing them again.

She read every account she could find about dead people who had reappeared to their loved ones.

In dreams. As apparitions. The black butterfly who fluttered around a woman's face as she left the hospital where her mother had just died. The same black butter-fly, or another one, appeared the next day in the woman's yard and didn't leave until the first snow.

The woman had never seen a butterfly like that before, anywhere. It had to be her mother, telling her she was all right.

The stray dog who showed up the day after a couple's young child died in a shooting. That dog seemed to know them, to know the house. He trotted right upstairs and settled into the boy's old bedroom before the couple realized what was happening.

They called it by their boy's name. The dog came running.

So many stories. Alice wanted to believe them all.

For too long she indulged in irrational hope. She sank into a fantasy life, searching everywhere for some sign that her mother and father were trying to reach out to her.

That they could hear her when she told them *I love you. I miss you.*

That they were somehow saying it back.

But after months of losing any sense of reality, months of complete immersion in this false and magical thinking, Alice realized it was eating away at her soul.

She had to stop. She had to wake up and move on.

She had to discover the truth about why they were dead.

Even now, she still kept a tight rein on her mind. If something wasn't real, if it wasn't true, she didn't want it.

But…

What would her parents say if they heard Major Zimholt's story?

Especially if they had watched with their own eyes as that alien device healed both his and Marnie's injuries?

Was Alice being rational now, or merely stubborn?

Sometimes she no longer knew the difference.

3

Once Major Zimholt was gone, Alice retreated to her own room.

She fell into a sleep that wasn't natural. She never slept during the day. She woke with a headache. She felt thirsty and hungry.

Her watch said 8:05. She assumed PM.

She knocked on Marnie's door. No answer.

Alice could hear voices coming from midway down the corridor. As she drew closer, she remembered it was a kitchen.

Three women and a man sat around a pale gray rectangular table. The women ate slices of pizza. Arnie Camper ate a big bowl of salad.

He smiled when he saw her. Alice lifted her hand in greeting. But she didn't want to join them. They all knew each other.

"Hungry?" Camper asked her.

The smell of the pizza almost drew her in. And they all had large bottles of water—she wanted that, too. Her headache was probably dehydration.

"No thanks," Alice said. "I have to find Marnie. Have you seen her?"

"Check the hangar," said the young black woman Alice had noticed earlier in the day.

The attractive young pilot who had grabbed Camper's arm and laughed at something he said.

The pilot reached into Camper's salad and popped one of his cherry tomatoes into her mouth. She grinned when he was too slow to stop her.

She looked younger than Alice, maybe in her early twenties. She wore her khaki, oversized coverall again. This close, Alice could read the nametag sewn on the left side of her chest. *Hix.*

"Thanks," Alice told her, then she hurried on. She didn't need to see anymore.

As she made her way back through the maze of corridors to where she thought she would find the hangar, she wondered if Marnie had eaten yet, either.

Dr. Sabbagh's warning rang in Alice's head.

You make her eat. She's not a lab rat, for godssake. She's as human as the rest of you.

Human though she was, Marnie was currently doing laps high above the concrete floor of the underground hangar, her arms gliding along in smooth strokes.

There were only a few workers beneath her this time of night, doing repairs on the pods in the first row.

Alice was surprised to see Major Zimholt over in the row, talking to one of the mechanics.

She wondered if he lived here, someplace inside the factory.

She hadn't given his personal life any thought at all until now.

He saw her and gave her a nod across the distance. After a short further discussion with the mechanic, Major Zimholt strode across the hangar to meet Alice.

He stood next to her and looked up to where Marnie was beginning another circuit.

"How long has she been here?" Alice asked.

"Half an hour or so."

"Did she have dinner?"

"You'll have to ask her."

Alice felt sheepish about her earlier behavior. She was grateful to Major Zimholt for giving her and Marnie a place to stay—a place to hide.

"Sir, I hope I wasn't too disrespectful. All my questions—"

He waved her concern away. "You're an analyst. I would expect no less. Which reminds me. There's a computer lab on the second floor, room two-eighty-two.

I've told them to expect you tomorrow. You're welcome to continue your research there."

Alice closed her eyes and breathed out a quiet sigh.

Then this wasn't a trick. He would do what he promised.

Alice had been cut off from the Agency's files for days now, since accessing them seemed to bring the assassins straight to her.

"And no one will be able to trace me?"

"We have our own system," said Major Zimholt. "It is completely internal to this mountain."

It meant that Alice could continue searching for answers, not only about her parents, but now about the attempts on her own life as well.

She was back on solid footing.

No talk of aliens. Back to her familiar world of human violence and crime.

And yet...

As she watched Marnie arc her arms through the air, doing butterfly, saw her restored ankle kick behind her next to the other one, Alice could not ignore her own hypocrisy.

She accepted these facts as real now. She knew that what she saw was true.

Marnie could fly. That neon-green beam of light had healed her ankle. Major Zimholt no longer had to wear a sling on his arm. Whatever its origin, alien or otherwise, the beam of light had healed the bullet wound to his shoulder.

The words escaped her before Alice could stop them.

"I don't know what to think anymore."

Major Zimholt chuckled. "I don't blame you. But tomorrow will be better already. I find that newcomers only need a few days. You'll be amazed at how quickly you adapt."

Alice turned and looked up at him. He met her image of a tall, distinguished old soldier. She wondered why he was only a major, and not a colonel or even a general. But maybe he had retired to the private sector before the military could raise him further in rank.

"So what do I do?" Alice asked him. It was the kind of question she rarely asked anyone. She had decided on her own path several years ago, and had relentlessly pursued it since then.

Major Zimholt didn't answer right away. Alice took it to mean that he gave her question serious consideration. She appreciated that.

"My father once told me," he said at last, "that our lives are as personal as we make them. As small or large as we make them. That the choice is ours."

Alice could see Marnie in the distance, beginning her descent. She must have flown enough to satisfy the urge for a while.

Alice would make sure they both ate soon. Maybe pizza, salad, and water.

But for now, she hoped Marnie would take her time coming over to join them. Alice wanted to hear what Major Zimholt had to say.

"He could have remained a simple mathematician," he went on. "My father had already played his part in this world, being a soldier in the German army. He could have led a simple life once he escaped with my mother and me to America.

"But he couldn't rest with himself if he did that. He had seen too much evil." Major Zimholt's voice softened. "We all had."

Alice had a flash then, of buildings being bombed. Of gunfire strafing a city block. Of old people, women, and children—citizens, not soldiers—falling to the pavement, their bodies bloodied.

Was it some movie she had once seen? No more than a product of her imagination?

But something about Major Zimholt's face now—his clenched jaw, the haunted look in his eyes—told Alice this man had experienced for himself the horrors of war. Not one fought overseas, in some other country, but one that raged right on his doorstep. On his own streets.

He must have been only a young child then.

How much had that young boy seen?

Alice could easily imagine the carnage that day when the gunman killed both her parents and the other inno-cent people standing with them in the crowd.

But she didn't *see* it. What if she had? Would her eyes

have that same sad and haunted look that she saw in Major Zimholt's gaze right now?

Alice understood what Major Zimholt's father must have meant. About our lives being as personal as we make them.

As small or as large as we make them.

Alice's life had been very specific for a while now.

Find the people behind her parents' murder.

Hunt them down. Expose them.

Kill them if the opportunity came to her. If she was sure, if she really *knew*, then she wouldn't take the chance of them escaping someone else's more formal justice.

She would wield justice herself.

But was that enough?

Was that all she was supposed to do?

Was that what Major Zimholt was trying to tell her?

He looked down at her now, met her gaze. The pain in his eyes was gone. In its place was a look of sympathy. As though Alice's pain was much greater than his.

"You do important work at the Agency," said Major Zimholt. "I have no doubt. You do your part to fight the evil that you see.

"But there is so much more. So much you don't see. Not yet."

Alice's pulse quickened. "What do you mean?"

Marnie was almost here. Alice needed the answer now.

Major Zimholt cupped his hands together tightly.

"There is the evil we know because it has hurt us. The death of your parents. These men who have tried to kill you."

He loosened his hands and opened his fingers to form a larger sphere, the size of a grapefruit.

"Criminal enterprises. The Nazis. The mob. Larger, and seemingly more dangerous, but still only a fraction of the whole."

He expanded his hands out further.

"Governments. Nations."

He widened his hands again. "Worlds."

And there it was. Now he had gone too far. "You mean the aliens," Alice said, making no attempt to hide her disappointment.

She was with him until then. She could feel the allure of a greater cause than her own personal vendetta, but not if it meant believing in something so extreme.

She had real criminals to find. Real murderers to pursue.

She couldn't afford the luxury of imagining other foes from other worlds.

What was she supposed to do, trade in her gun for a blaster and chase bad aliens across the galaxy?

"No, Alice," said Major Zimholt. "I'm speaking of evil. The web of it that pervades all of our lives, whether we know who is behind it or not.

"Some people prefer not to see it. But for those who are willing..."

Marnie was here now. Major Zimholt shifted to his left to include her in their circle.

"For those who are willing," he said to them both, "we devote our lives to doing whatever we can to tear out that evil from the root. It is dangerous and thankless work. There are few victories. But when the victories come…"

His eyes seemed to burn with an inner light.

"When I do die," he said, "I will know that I did absolutely everything I could. And that… that is all I can ever ask for."

He gave them both a respectful and dignified nod.

Then Major Zimholt strode back to the row of pods and the mechanics who were toiling to fix them.

Marnie's cheeks looked flushed from her flight.

She gave Alice a puzzled but genuine smile.

"What do you think?" Marnie asked, still a little breathless from her exertion. "Of this place?"

Major Zimholt's words reverberated in Alice's head. She wasn't sure what she thought.

"What about you?" Alice asked instead.

Marnie nodded. "It's good. I think it's good."

Alice stared after the Major.

"Then maybe we should stay a while," she told Marnie. "And see."

FINDER

1

"Do you believe in evil?" Mrs. Byers asked.

Not a crazy question, Investigator Gina Firenzi thought, considering where they were.

A rundown shack of a house sitting on an acre of what was probably two million dollars worth of prime beachfront land. The shooter's parents owned the house, bought it thirty years before when the values were low.

The house stood out, the only tear-down not torn down. The couple who owned it, neighbors said, were awful. Difficult. Combative.

The couple's son lived in the shed in their back yard, and he was worse.

The parents were dead now. Shot by the son.

Along with thirty-six people at an outdoor New Year's Eve party.

It made Gina sick in her heart.

"I don't mean just criminality," Mrs. Byers said. "I mean true human evil. You must see that sometimes in your work."

"I don't know," Gina said. "I don't usually go there."

"Yes," Mrs. Byers agreed. "It's a black hole."

Mrs. Byers was an elegant lady. Early seventies, with long white hair piled into a neat topknot, ironed navy blue slacks, a red Christmas sweater. She had a slight curvature of her shoulders that made her look shorter than she probably was. At five-eleven Gina felt like she towered over her.

"Posture," Gina's mother always used to remind her, poking her in the back. By the time Gina was in junior high, she was already the tallest kid in her school. But she was never allowed to slouch.

Mrs. Byers also wore a pretty gray crocheted scarf that she probably crocheted herself. She reminded Gina of her own Nana. A nice old lady to be in such a horrible place.

Gina checked her watch. "We should go in."

Mrs. Byers sighed. "Yes."

It was late afternoon on New Year's Day, sixteen hours after the shooting. They were on a short clock. The house was set to be demolished at eight AM the following morning, just as soon as everyone was working again after the holiday.

"Why the rush?" Gina had asked her supervisor. "Don't you think that's strange?"

"For the sake of the grieving families..." went the official explanation. *"No one wants a monument to the killer."*

Gina's supervisor didn't buy the official line either. He made some calls, made a deal, and bought Gina just two hours in the house to find out whatever she could.

This wasn't supposed to be the Agency's case. The visit would have to remain unofficial. In two hours someone from law enforcement would show up and take away the key.

It wasn't the first time Gina had to go through the dance. She didn't care as long as she got what she needed.

She unlocked the door and stepped inside. And immediately smelled the crazy.

The reek of garbage and rotting food. Of toilets inadequately flushed. Of body odor so overwhelming it was as if it had been slathered all over the furniture.

The living room looked filthy, crap everywhere, not like someone had tossed the place, but just because these people were pigs.

Gina covered her nose with her sleeve. Mrs. Byers held her pretty gray scarf across her face.

"What do you need from me?" Gina asked her.

"Nothing," Mrs. Byers answered. "You go about your business. I'll go about mine."

Mrs. Byers surveyed the state of the couch. There

were dirty clothes, a soiled blanket, crusty food containers piled all over it. The single chair in the room looked stained with urine.

"Actually," Mrs. Byers said, "a roll of paper towels would be nice."

"Sure thing," said Gina, and set off for the kitchen to find them.

The kitchen was far worse.

A sink full of plates caked in rotting food. A rancid stench coming from the fridge. Empty takeout containers all over the counters and on the floor. Open microwave with chunks of food splattered on the sides and door. Overflowing garbage can. Empty beer bottles and cans. Empty wine bottles. Stale smoke and two overflowing ashtrays.

The chaos and squalor. How did people live like this?

Because they're crazy. Did Gina believe in evil? No, but she believed in crazy.

There were no paper towels. She grabbed a short stack of napkins that must have come with one of the takeouts and brought them back to Mrs. Byers.

The older woman still wore her scarf across her mouth and nose. She had used some of the discarded Christmas paper wrapping in the corner near a fake tree to make herself a clean nest to sit on at the side of the couch.

"No paper towels," Gina said, offering Mrs. Byers the napkins.

"It's all right, dear. You'd best get on with your work." Mrs. Byers unzipped her small bulging purse and took out a pen and small spiral notebook. She opened to a fresh page, then she closed her eyes and settled in.

Gina had seen the process. She'd worked with her before. Mrs. Byers had called her *dear* then too.

Gina held the wad of thick napkins against her nose. Then she began taking a different kind of look around. Not as an ordinary citizen, appalled by how these people lived, but as a professional.

Law enforcement had already been through the place. She knew they probably took all the computers and any cell phones or other devices.

They would have searched all the rooms for weapons. Bomb-making equipment. Any of the usual things associated with shooters.

Also bank records, if there were any. Proof of large amounts of money coming in.

Looking around the house, Gina doubted that. But people were weird with their money. Just because they didn't spend it, didn't mean they didn't have it.

And Gina had a reason to wonder about the money.

A reason to wonder about this shooter's whole situation in general.

Just a few weeks ago Gina took a knife to her back from an attacker who meant to kill somebody else: one of the analysts at the Agency, a young woman called Alice Kern. Alice had already been attacked a few hours earlier by a man who broke into her apartment in the middle of the night.

Two attacks, both attackers killed in the attempt. Alice Kern had some hidden skills.

She also had extensive files that Gina had been delving into while she was supposed to be on leave, recuperating from the wound to her back.

Gina already knew that Alice's parents had been killed in a mass shooting about six years ago. There were notes in Alice's personnel file about whether that should be a concern in hiring her.

But her credentials were solid, excellent grades, outstanding references, and everything was fine with her psych profile. Alice was still fairly new at the job, but all the reports so far said she was a dedicated and hard worker who had a real talent for analysis.

What Gina didn't know before—and wondered whether anyone else did either—was that in addition to all of her assigned work, Alice had a side project going.

It hadn't been easy for Gina to find. But she saw a stray set of data in one of Alice's many files, and was curious enough to pull on that string. She kept following it over a course of days until finally she discovered where it led.

Gina had no idea where Alice found enough time to do as much as she did, but there it was, a database she had created going back at least fifteen years, listing as many details as she could find about mass shootings all around the country.

Age of the killers. Where they lived. Family background. Schooling. Criminal records. Known associates. Financial situation. Unusually large bank deposits. Hobbies. Gaming habits. Social media accounts. On and on and on.

Gina had a rule about turning off her work at night and keeping a clear head so she could fall asleep. It was also so she could keep doing this job that she loved without burning out like so many other people did. So it took her over a week of continuous daytime reading before she could review all of Alice's database.

And it was while Alice's different data points still swarmed in Gina's head that the New Year's Eve shooter had murdered all those people.

Something about the case.

The demolition.

Gina saw some reference to it on the news and immediately knew where she'd seen that before.

More than once, in fact. Multiple times.

"For the sake of the families... So the neighbors don't have to walk by it every day... Remove the stain..."

A mass shooting, the shooter killed, whether by law enforcement or self-inflicted, and then shortly after, usually within forty-eight hours, the shooter's house razed to the ground.

Alice had listed the demolition companies. A different

company name in every case, different companies in different states—but almost all of them owned by the same parent corporation out of Florida.

And it wasn't for lack of choice. Alice had researched that as well. She listed all the other demolition companies in or near the relevant cities and towns. There were plenty of local construction companies that did demolition too.

Why should a shooter's house in Iowa be demolished by a company that drove in from Nevada? Especially when there were at least five other Iowa demolition companies within a few hundred miles of the house?

Who decided which company got hired?

There were no records of formal bids in any of the files Alice reviewed. No reason why one parent company in Florida should be given the almost exclusive job of rushing in and razing all these mass murderers' houses.

So Gina had done the same analysis, as soon as she heard about this house.

Found out who was supposed to do the demolition, then looked up the business's filings with the state of California. Kept following the trail, subsidiary to another corporation and another, until finally she drilled down to that same parent company in Florida.

It simply couldn't be a coincidence.

What it meant, though, Gina still had no clue. Looking at Alice's notes, it didn't seem like Alice had the answers either.

But Gina thought it was enough to take to her own supervisor.

"You're supposed to still be out for another week," he said when she called.

"Yeah, well."

She didn't tell him everything, not yet. Gina still wasn't sure what to do about that. She couldn't swear that Alice was authorized to research what she'd been researching. Some of it was in Agency files even Gina had to go through channels to access. She doubted that a one-year analyst had the clout to go straight in.

It might be more of Alice's hidden skills. Some sort of ninja work with computers.

But Gina liked Alice. She had no need to get her into trouble. Alice had saved Gina's life. Even though her life might never have been in danger if Alice wasn't doing whatever she was doing.

Was Alice's research the reason why two men had tried to kill her? Did it have anything to do with this latest shooting?

Who else knew about Alice's database? Was it someone at the Agency? Who did that person tell?

And why all these demolitions? That was a piece of the puzzle that nagged at Gina, the same way it must have at Alice.

It couldn't be to destroy computer hard drives or weapons or anything else that law enforcement would normally seize from inside a house. All of those would have been gone within hours after the killer was first identified.

So it had to be something about the houses themselves.

But what?

That's what she hoped Mrs. Byers could help her find out.

Nobody had bothered cleaning the blood and gore off the parents' bed. That would have required a separate call to a separate unit, and maybe by then they knew everything was going to be turned into splinters and dust by the demolition equipment, so why bother tidying up?

Gina held the wad of napkins harder against her nose and mouth. She didn't want to even accidentally breathe in the smell. She knew she should go in, look around, lift things, look under things, but she couldn't bring herself to do it.

Soft, she scolded herself.

She'd own that.

But there was no one around she had to impress, and

she needed to be mindful of her time. The son lived in the shed out back. She should focus her attention there.

She turned from the bedroom where the son had shot his parents while they slept. In the early hours of New Year's Eve, as near as they could tell. Then he let them lie there all day and into the evening while he finished whatever preparations he made to go out in time to shoot up the party at midnight.

Gina bypassed the fetid bathroom off the hall. No point in subjecting herself to whatever horrors were in there. She could already smell a preview, even through the filter of the napkins.

There was another smaller bedroom past the hall bathroom. The door was open. She glanced in. Storage, if you could call it that. Junk piled on top of junk. Broken furniture. Empty boxes. Papers, what looked like bills. The kind of things someone could go through at their leisure once the cleaning crew boxed them up, but no one was going to waste their time now.

She followed the rest of the dirty brown carpet to the door at the end of the hall. Used the edge of her shirt to turn the knob. Not to preserve any fingerprints, but to stop getting any more of these people's filth on her. She'd forgotten to bring gloves. Once she got the okay, she'd been in such a hurry to pick up Mrs. Byers and drive the two hours out to this beach, she'd forgotten to pack any of her normal equipment.

Just a few weeks rest from the job and already she'd gotten sloppy.

Gina opened the door and stepped out into the scruffy dirt lot that passed for their back yard. She could hear the surf. She imagined this would be a nice spot to live if you had a pretty house.

More broken junk out here. Motorcycle parts. Upholstered chairs with holes in the arms and seats. A broken clothes line. A couple of old and sun-bleached surfboards. A long rickety-looking wooden ramp someone had put up for skateboarding. More loose garbage.

This whole place was depressing.

Not as depressing as what he did.

In front of Gina was a wooden shed up against the chain link fence that surrounded the yard. The shed might have been sturdy once, twenty years ago, but now the door was sagging on its hinges and wood had rotted off parts of the roof and along the sides.

Law enforcement had broken off the bicycle lock used to secure the door. Now the door gaped open, showing off an interior completely unlike the house.

Sparse. Orderly. Clean.

Gina's gut clenched. A different side of crazy.

She kicked the door all the way open and peered inside. The day was still bright enough that she could see most of what was there.

A twin bed, neatly made, a threadbare ivory-colored

bedspread on top. Pillow smoothed out and positioned perfectly at the head of the bed.

A U-shaped desk. Gina could see loose cords hanging down. They would have belonged to computers and computer screens. It looked like there might have been one each on all three surfaces of the U.

A desk chair with a clean black cushion on the seat.

A stack of two white wooden cubes with their openings facing out, and neatly folded inside them various T-shirts and other clothes.

A pair of very clean white sneakers lined up neatly in front of them.

Gina stood at the door of the shed taking it all in.

It was like a show. Like something fake. Some movie designer's version of a mass murderer's monk-like room.

She didn't understand it at all.

There was a single shelf above the desk and a few books neatly lined up there, propped between cheap metal bookends.

A hardback set of a thriller trilogy Gina remembered hearing about a few years ago, but never read. Also a thick paperback about computer graphics and another about designing code.

The only thing that didn't fit with the picture she was seeing of a clean and orderly life was the smell wafting toward her from the left. Like a dog yard someone never hosed down. The reek of urine was unmistakable.

There's no bathroom, Gina realized. No toilet, no sink, no plumbing.

The shooter would have had to go back into the house for any of that.

So he just peed onto the dirt outside. Maybe did more. She wasn't going to look.

"I'm ready," Mrs. Byers said.

The older woman stood at the doorway leading back into the house, still holding the crocheted scarf against her face.

"Come outside," Gina asked her. "I want you to take a look at this."

3

Mrs. Byers sat gingerly on the edge of the twin bed. She had ripped off the top three sheets of paper from her notebook and handed them to Gina. Now she lifted her pen to a blank piece of paper once more and closed her eyes.

Gina stepped outside to look at the drawings.

She recognized the first as the living room. None of the details drawn in, none of the squalor, but Mrs. Byers had sketched the room's shape. One opening toward the kitchen, another toward the hallway.

Mrs. Byers had drawn little circles in various spots. She drew arrows from each of them all pointing at one word: *Camera.*

Gina's nerves buzzed. She would have to go back inside the house.

The second sheet of paper showed a camera in the kitchen. The third, in the master bedroom.

If they were on, still running, still recording—

Gina couldn't let them see that she knew.

The easiest might be in the kitchen. The living room had too many. Gina walked back up the hallway, ignoring the master bedroom for now, turned left into the living room, left again into the kitchen.

She kept her head down, pretending to examine the table. According to Mrs. Byers's drawing, the camera was above the refrigerator. It could have a wide view of the whole room from there. It might be hard to get behind it. Gina stole a look at the fridge. Maybe if she pulled it out.

Using a couple of unused napkins she picked off the floor, she opened the handle of the refrigerator and pretended to look inside. The stench was overpowering. She held her sleeve against her nose.

She tested the weight of the fridge. Pulled on the door and the other side wall to see if it had enough give. She might be able to move it by herself, but it would take time. There was no casual way of pulling it out so she could slip into the space behind it and look up to find where the camera was hidden.

She retreated back into the dark hallway. There were no cameras here, at least none that Mrs. Byers noted, so Gina stood and looked at the other drawings.

The one in the parents' bedroom was above their closet, aimed toward the bed.

Maybe that one would be easier after all.

She stepped back into the master bedroom, both blocking her nose and holding her breath. The closet had two sliding mirrored doors. Gina slid open the nearest side.

There was a lightbulb inside the closet. She found the switch and flipped it on. Then standing inside the closet she looked up all along the top edge of the door to see if she could find any wires. A battery-operated camera would be less conspicuous, but someone would have to freshen the batteries now and then. If they could hard wire it, they only had to mess with it once.

There. She saw it. The wire was thin, painted white like the rest of the wall, but if you looked for it you could see it.

It disappeared into the drywall above the track where the doors had to slide. Gina was tall, but not that tall. She needed to stand on something.

Could she risk bringing in one of the chairs from the kitchen? If someone were watching her right now, what would they think?

Still standing inside the open closet, Gina looked out into the parents' bedroom. Two bedside tables, too hard to move. No books she could stack, these people weren't readers.

The clothes. They would have to be good enough.

Gina turned around and pulled everything off the hangers. Coats, shirts, pants, every single thing. She wrapped shoes inside of clothes, building sets of higher layers. Finally she had a fairly solid stack that she could stand on to gain the necessary inches.

She used the hook from a wire hanger to start digging into the drywall. Finally she made a hole large enough that she could see the back of the camera.

A green light on the back told her it was on.

Gina's heart sped.

Who's watching? Who are these people?

She left everything where it was, including her makeshift stool. She closed the closet door and escaped back into the hall.

She could feel her pulse pounding in the side of her neck.

She checked her watch. They were running out time.

She didn't bother trying to look for the cameras in the living room. She knew they were there.

Mrs. Byers had proven herself reliable the last time Gina worked with her. Some in the Agency doubted the Finders' skills, thought it was all mystical bull, but Gina was more practical than that.

She didn't doubt there were people with special abilities. There was even a branch of the Agency set aside right now to help those people develop their skills. Not everybody knew about it, but Gina knew.

So when she heard about the Finders, she read through their files. Talked to some of the agents involved. Read about the two decades of incredible discoveries Mrs. Byers and other Finders in the program had made until for whatever reason the new Agency director at the time decided to shut the program down.

But those people were still out there, Gina learned. Many of them, like Mrs. Byers, were still eager and willing to help.

Whatever works. Gina would take every advantage she could get. If it meant fewer bad guys out in the world, she'd learn voodoo if she had to.

So she'd contacted Mrs. Byers, sat down with her in her bright pretty kitchen, ate Mrs. Byers's homemade pumpkin bread and drank her peach-flavored tea.

"We're not special," Mrs. Byers had explained. "Anyone can do it. You just have to decide you can."

But even if Gina had decided it was within her power to find a certain stash of files and photographs she'd been tipped off were hidden in a particular warehouse, three weeks of searching for them on her own had gotten her nowhere.

So she brought in Mrs. Byers. And had the treasure in hand within an hour.

"Think of when you're driving your car," Mrs. Byers had tried to explain. "Your sense of your personal space expands to include the whole car. You know when someone is driving too close. You can feel it and you swerve to get away. You know how wide you have to turn to avoid a curb. You have become, for a time, your car."

She had laughed at the skeptical expression on Gina's face.

"It's just the same as when you're talking to a stranger," Mrs. Byers went on, "and the person moves in too close. Don't you automatically feel it?"

"Yes…"

"We all have an innate sense of our personal space," said Mrs. Byers. "What they taught us in the program was how to expand how much our personal space can include."

It was why, she said, she could sit inside a building and know things about what she would find in all the rooms.

"That building is me," Mrs. Byers said. "For as long as I want it to be." She smiled and patted Gina's hand. "You seem a lovely, smart girl. You should try it for yourself, dear."

Now that elegant old lady sat on a killer's bed in a ramshackle shed in the fading light.

Gina had left her alone out there too long.

And they were almost out of time.

Other than finding the camera in the closet, Gina thought as she strode back out of the filthy house, she had no new information to show for it.

4

Mrs. Byers stood outside the shed. The gray crocheted scarf was off her face now and wrapped around her neck. She hugged her arms against her chest.

"Cold?" Gina asked.

Mrs. Byers nodded but gave her a smile. She handed Gina another drawing. "We'll be finished soon enough."

A camera in the shed, it looked like somewhere above the bed, maybe aimed at where the shooter sat at his computers.

Gina tried to think of what was on that wall. She didn't want to go back inside to check and end up looking directly into the camera.

"How is it hidden?" she asked Mrs. Byers. The walls were bare wood, no drywall to cut a hole in and patch.

"It's high in a dark corner," Mrs. Byers answered. "You could find it if you shined a flashlight."

Gina looked at the drawing again. Mrs. Byers had drawn a small square behind the outline of the shed.

"What's this?" Gina asked.

Mrs. Byers pointed to the left of the shed, where the urine smell was strongest.

Gina held her sleeve against her nose and walked over.

She peered behind the shed. She had thought before that it sat flush against the chain link fence, but now she saw there was a narrow space.

She walked closer. She could see something on the ground, hidden behind the shed.

It looked like a dirty blanket.

Mrs. Byers now stood by her side. "It's there," she said. "Something underneath."

Again Gina wished she had gloves.

She kicked aside the blanket. There was nothing beneath it. She looked back at Mrs. Byers.

"Underneath the shed, I should think," she said.

Gina knelt at the corner of the shed and bent over to look beneath the wooden floor. She could see that a hole had been dug in the dirt there.

If she had more time, she could go get a flashlight. Buy some gloves. Use some sort of tool to fish the items out. But all she had were her bare hands and a few paper napkins.

She thought about asking Mrs. Byers if she could use her scarf, but that nice old lady had already done enough.

Gina bent low, trying to see, and used the napkins to begin pulling things out of the hole.

A hash pipe. A few porn magazines.

A small plastic bag with about twenty pale pink pills.

A knife in a stiff leather sheath.

A large plastic bag stuffed full with hundred dollar bills.

Two pens. A small leather bound notebook.

Gina felt in the hole once more, assuring herself she'd gotten it all.

Did the shooter know about the camera in his shed?

Did he come sit on a blanket back here and get high and jerk off to porn?

Where did he get the money? Why was he hiding it back here?

Gina flipped through the notebook. Pages and pages of nearly illegible scrawl. Handwriting that looked like it belonged back in that disordered house rather than in the neat monastic shed.

Ignoring her repulsion at having anything of the killer's touch her skin, Gina lifted her shirt and shoved the notebook down the waistband of her pants.

Whatever was in that notebook, it had been important enough to write.

And important enough to hide.

"Okay, it's time to go," she told Mrs. Byers.

She scooped up the other items and carried them loose in her arms. The money, the pills, the pipe, the knife. Even the porn magazines.

Gina and Mrs. Byers came around the side of the shed.

An officer waited in the yard.

Local, from the look of his uniform. Quiet. Gina never heard him.

"Evening," said Gina.

"Evening," the officer answered. He nodded to Mrs. Byers.

He looked young, late twenties, a little shorter and skinnier than Gina, but in good shape. Big biceps beneath the tight sleeves of his uniform.

The officer glanced at the load in Gina's arms. The bag of money was near the top.

There was a wind now coming up from the shore. Gina knew Mrs. Byers must be cold.

"I need to log these things in," said Gina. She kept her voice low and strong, the voice of authority.

"I'll take care of it," the officer said.

He was wearing his service weapon.

Gina was not wearing hers.

"Have you ever met someone new," Mrs. Byers had asked her while they ate pumpkin bread in her kitchen, *"and gotten the most horrible feeling? You can't say why, but you can't wait to get away."*

"Yes," Gina said. *"I've felt that."*

"It's your aura," Mrs. Byers said. *"Your aura fills your personal space. It can give you information. Sometimes another person is so awful, their aura extends out and bumps against yours even before you're close. You can feel it. Danger."*

Gina was feeling it now.

She breathed normally, steadily. Even though her heart had picked up speed. She planted her feet evenly and stood tall and erect, making herself as big as possible.

She could feel Mrs. Byers beside her, moving closer into Gina's space.

Gina had a responsibility to take care of Mrs. Byers. She couldn't do anything crazy.

"So what happens here?" Gina asked the officer, keeping her voice calm.

"I'll take care of that," he said again, gesturing toward her arms.

"Sure," said Gina. She kept her eyes on the officer as she lowered the pile to the ground.

She pretended to lose her grip for a moment. The pile shifted. She stacked the items neatly again.

Then she straightened back up, hugging her arms across her chest the way Mrs. Byers had before.

"It's cold," Gina told the man. "I need to get my Nana home."

There was no gate leading out of the chain link. She would have preferred to go that way. Instead Gina freed one of her hands to take gentle hold of Mrs. Byers's elbow and began leading the old woman toward the house.

Gina could feel the officer following. She stole enough of a glance to see that he left the pile in the yard.

That was both good for her and bad.

Good because he hadn't examined the items.

Bad because he was now behind them.

Back inside the dark hallway, Gina didn't bother covering her nose. She guided Mrs. Byers to walk in front of her. The hall was too narrow for them to walk together.

Even without looking, Gina could feel where the officer was. His presence was palpable, like a loud and throbbing heartbeat she could feel vibrating against her skin.

When he moved, she moved.

She twisted in place, knife in her hand, and thrust it hard into his chest. He held the gun, it was up and aimed at her, but she shoved his arm into the wall.

"RUN!" she shouted at Mrs. Byers.

The officer punched Gina in the head.

Her vision blurred. But it didn't matter. She held on to him and knew where he was.

Gina slammed her elbow against his face and rammed his body against the wall.

The knife was still in his chest. She knew what that felt like now. The pain of it, the invasion, even though her attacker's knife had barely stayed in her for a second.

Gina pressed her left forearm tight against the offi-cer's throat, holding him against the wall. Then with her right hand she grabbed the handle of the knife, pulled it out, and stabbed again.

Blood flowed warm across her fingers. The officer shouted. Tried to break free.

Tears streamed down Gina's face. She had never killed a man like this. Close up. Breathing his breath. It made her sick. She had to do it.

His legs started to buckle. Gina kept her forearm strong and tight across his throat. It didn't matter whether it was the knife or her arm, she needed him to stop breathing one way or another.

She was sweating. Panting. She remembered to look for the gun. It had fallen a few feet back. She would grab it right now if it were close.

But she was afraid to let go. Afraid to give him a single inch. Until she knew the threat was over. Until she knew both she and Mrs. Byers were safe.

The officer sagged. No fight left at all. Gina kept her arm in place and used her free hand to check for a pulse at the side of his neck.

Then she finally let him go.

He fell to the ground. She picked up the gun.

When she looked up, Mrs. Byers was there, watching from the end of the hall.

Her hands were gripped tight together in front of her

face, pressed against her lips, like a woman saying her prayers.

Her wide eyes met Gina's.

"We need to leave," said Gina. "Now."

She had no idea what sounds the cameras picked up. It was possible other people were coming soon.

She kept the gun in her hand but hid it behind her bent other arm. Mrs. Byers stayed close, practically leaning on Gina, as the two of them left the house.

It was dark now, not pitch, but dark enough that Gina had to squint to look around. The officer's car was there, but parked further down the dirt road that led to the house. He hadn't wanted her to hear him. It worked. Gina didn't.

It was an ordinary sedan anyone might have. Not a police cruiser.

He might not be police at all. She already doubted, back there in the yard.

She unlocked her doors with the remote, then opened the passenger side and helped Mrs. Byers in.

Gina continued scanning the area. Her senses were still on alert. Her pounding pulse agreed it wasn't time to let her guard down.

Gina got in the car, locked the doors, started the car and drove away.

She pulled the killer's notebook out of her waistband and threw it onto her back seat. She kept the gun at her side.

Then she handed her phone to Mrs. Byers and told her which number to call.

"There's a body," Gina told her supervisor. "It might not be there very long. There are cameras. They probably know. Get someone over as soon as you can."

She drove twenty miles before she believed they were away free.

Mrs. Byers was still shuddering beside her.

Gina reached over and squeezed her hand.

There in her car, driving toward a dark freeway, Gina understood what Mrs. Byers meant. About how your sense of yourself can expand. How you can fill all the space around you.

Fill it, and feel it.

Gina could feel the two lives inside that car, both their hearts still beating, alive.

Could feel what it meant to protect them. To decide no matter what, she wouldn't lose.

Gina let out a long, slow breath.

Her hand was filthy, coated in blood.

Mrs. Byers still squeezed it. Hard.

FLIER

1

Marnie jogged up the wide metal stairs to the thick metal door leading outside.

It was just dawn. No one saw her leave. Not because of the flight suit that made her invisible when she flew—it was hidden right now beneath a puffy charcoal-colored down coat and navy blue sweatpants—but because she knew how to be silent and smooth whenever she slipped away. She had been practicing for over eleven years.

Normally Alice came with her whenever Marnie wanted to go topside. Alice claimed to love the cold crisp air and the spectacular view of the snow-capped mountains surrounding them on every side, but Marnie knew it was for protection. Marnie wasn't strong even at her best, and she was still recovering from her concussion and the bruising to her ribs.

Dr. Caroline Baird had fixed Marnie's ankle, but said she didn't want to risk the beam around any of Marnie's internal organs. And certainly not her brain.

But the healed ankle was enough of a gift. Marnie had seen Dr. Baird once since then, a few days ago, and thanked her again profusely.

Marnie looked around them in the corridor to make sure no one else could hear.

Then she asked, "Is it really alien?"

Dr. Baird adjusted her thick glasses and gave a solemn nod. "It really is."

Marnie felt a wash of that same, strange joy, flooding through her veins.

Aliens. The future. Some advanced race. Something above and beyond what sometimes felt so dark and primitive about the human race.

It reminded Marnie of that first night in the Alaskan wilderness when she beat her arms hard against the cold air and felt her feet rising from the snow.

January 4. Twelve years ago today.

Always a sad day in memory, not one to celebrate.

But Marnie could admit to herself now, here, after what she had seen and heard inside the Factory over the past week, that she had felt otherworldly back then, that first extraordinary night.

Like an alien herself. Or maybe just more, more than simply human.

She had looked down at the snow-covered clearing and seen her mother staring in wonder high up where Marnie flew.

The way earthlings stare up at the stars. Wondering what mysteries space might hold. What miraculous and spectacular secrets.

Wondering if they, the mortals here on Earth, might ever touch the sparkling stars and the glowing planets, either while alive or after they died.

Marnie remembered a moment of wondering that herself, the higher she climbed that first night she flew.

Would she die up here? Would she disappear into the black void of the heavens? Would the stars absorb her, swallow her whole?

Marnie almost wished that the cluster of lights above her would take her in and keep her forever.

She wasn't suicidal. It wasn't a death wish. Instead she felt overcome by an inspired and joyful yearning.

It was only afterward that she felt the weight of what she had become. The burden of the new compulsion that would never go away.

The separation between her and the rest of the normal human race.

The separation between her and the mother she loved.

Marnie pushed down on the lever handle of the heavy metal door, and shouldered it open to venture outside.

It had snowed overnight. A fresh layer of soft, powdery white covered the earth around her, forming round pillows around even the roughest of rocks.

She wore thick snow boots, lined in fleece, that Major Zimholt had had someone bring to Marnie's room the day after she and Alice arrived.

And other warm clothes for both of them. As though acknowledging their decision to stay for a while.

Marnie unzipped her down coat and spread it on the ground. She removed her boots and the sweatpants and set them on top, and wrapped them all up in a bundle. She stowed them at the base of a blue spruce tree nearby. Then she swung her arms in a circle to warm up.

She wore one of the warmer, thicker flight suits Major Zimholt gave her. She had already tucked in her hair and snugged the hood of it around her face back inside the Factory.

She pulled the sleeves down low across her hands and slipped her thumbs into the holes made for them to keep the sleeve ends in place.

The flight suit was all one piece that covered her feet as well. The soles bore some kind of rougher material to give her some traction.

Her ribs still ached if she overextended her arms, but doing these warm-ups loosened some of the pain and stiffness.

Within five minutes of stepping through the door to the outside, Marnie ran across the snow and lifted into the air.

She could feel the frozen crystals inside the wind. It wasn't snowing, but the air was so cold.

Her breath fogged and froze in front of her.

The frigid air froze the hairs in her nose.

She breathed through her mouth mostly, and even then she thought she caught the scent of pine needles in the forest below.

From up here she could see the tracks of various animals in the snow. The small ones must be foxes. The largest ones elk.

Marnie felt no hurry, no urgency. She might fly for hours if she wanted to. The suit kept her warm and invisible.

No one asked anything of her here. No one seemed to keep track of her, except maybe Alice.

It was better than at the Aviary. There, Marnie knew that people followed her on her flights, staying high above, and filming what she did.

She was always waiting for the day when Ted Whitling or someone else would tell her that was enough, it was time to start earning her keep.

Marnie never doubted that the military or the government would find some special use for her.

But she always knew she would bolt before they used her against her will.

She was always poised, ready to flee.

But it felt different here. She and Alice had been at the Factory for over a week now, and Marnie had stopped wondering when anyone would come and try to force her to do anything she didn't want to do.

She assumed it was because of Major Zimholt. He was a man of honor. A man of his word.

He offered Marnie and Alice sanctuary, no strings attached.

Here at the start of her twelfth year of it, Marnie might be through with running.

2

S harman Hix nosed her pod to the right. She caught herself moving her head, and cursed under her breath.

It was like catching herself moving her lips when she was reading when she was a kid.

Just a habit, and one she finally broke.

She rolled her shoulders to relax again. Tilted her head to the right and left, heard her neck crack.

She took a deep breath and started again. *Left. Right. Up.*

The pod responded smoothly. Sharman smiled. She was back on track.

She wiggled her bare toes against the skin of the control pad. The craft picked up speed, just as she asked it to in her mind.

She was one with this machine. It was part of her body now. An extension of her limbs, an extension of her mind.

She held her head steady, wouldn't allow it to move even an inch, as she thought, *Roll now, nice and smooth.*

When she was a rookie she used to go through all sorts of contortions. The rolls were especially embarrassing. She'd jerk her head to the right, drop her right shoulder, practically throw all of her weight against the controls.

It only took a few times of hearing her instructors' laughter through her headset for her to cure herself of the habit, just out of plain anger and pride.

No one ever laughed at her now. Sharman Hix was Senior Pilot First Class, the youngest ever named. She was twenty-four now, and had held the distinction for two years.

She knew this pod—any of the pods—like she knew her own fingers and toes. It was why she flew barefoot, when no one else did.

She liked to feel skin against skin, even though the pod's controls were more solid than pliable flesh and at times uncomfortably cold once they left the hangar.

But Sharman wanted as little between her and the controls as she could get.

When she climbed into one of the pods and placed her feet up on the angled platform, and slid her arms against the arms of her chair, she liked to press her fingerprints and footprints against the machine.

Hey, it's me. Let's show 'em how it's done.

She swore the pods reacted differently whenever she was at the controls.

She had never yet have one break down on her. Some of the other pilots seemed to go through pods like they thought they were disposable. *Just get me another, this one doesn't work.*

A lot of them washed out of the program pretty fast.

The ones who stayed had to prove themselves to Sharman. Major Zimholt trusted her to build the kind of team that he needed.

She was young, but she had been with the program since the day she turned eighteen. Six years with more flights to her credit than anyone else.

And she was *good*. Excellent. Better than any of them. Age didn't have anything to do with that.

It was a matter of feel. And yeah, nerve. You couldn't be a chicken and take one of these pods out for a spin. Not with all the crazy air currents around all these mountains, pushing the pods this way and that, and if you lose your bearings, you're good as done.

There were four in a row like that, all in the same month, slamming into the rocks and never heard from again.

It shook her. Sharman went to Zimholt and told him what she knew.

Those pilots were no good. She could see it the first time they flew. They didn't have the feel for it. They didn't have the right minds. She could have told him they wouldn't make it, and she felt like crap that she hadn't spoken up.

Zimholt put her in charge after that. No one wanted more deaths. And there hadn't been any more until last year.

Just one, but it was like a punch to Sharman's chest. She had ignored what her gut was telling her.

The pilot was experienced. Enthusiastic. Maybe a little bit arrogant. She seemed to have what it took.

She flew Snack Packs with Arnie Camper over at the Aviary. He vouched for her that she was even better than him.

But the pods weren't like the Snack Packs or any other crafts, even the experimental ones. The pods were different.

They were more like riding a horse, Sharman told the new pilots their first days. They were *alive*. You had to respect the pods and treat them like partners.

The ones who got it, loved it. Loved it *hard*. Sharman could usually tell in the first fifteen minutes whether the pilots were a match.

Like trusting your dog to growl if some stranger isn't right.

To wag his tail if the person was solid.

Sharman let the pods tell her as much about the pilots as the pilots tried to tell her themselves.

If the pods wouldn't fly right for them, then the pilots were out.

All the men and women she had on her team right now seemed the right fit, even if some of them were still learning.

When they got to the point where their pods never broke down on them again, Sharman would know the pilots were ready to graduate to the next part of their mission.

3

Marnie alighted sometimes on the edges of cliffs. She needed to get over this. It was the only way to do it.

Alice was right. The more ways that Marnie could take off if she needed to escape, the safer she would be. It was why Alice was still working with her to strengthen the muscles in her legs so Marnie could take off vertically, jumping straight up from the ground.

There wasn't a trampoline here where Marnie could practice her vertical leaps, but there were plenty of gyms scattered all over the Factory where Alice could show Marnie how to work out.

Squats and lunges, leg lifts with the machines, even time on the treadmill, although Marnie soon argued her way out of that.

She would rather hike up the metal stairs or go outside and march through the snow than put up with the monotony of just walking in place.

But Marnie could already feel the difference. Her legs were getting stronger. She could feel it every time she ran and leapt into one of her takeoffs.

But what if she were ever injured again? What if she couldn't run?

It was time to give up the decision she had made long ago.

She knew it when she first entered the Factory and removed the hard plastic boot and flew down to the foot of the staircase.

And after that, when Christopher drove one of the transports over, and carried Marnie up to the ceiling of the hangar so she could dive off the edge.

She could feel the cold sweat break out on her face. But she needed to fly, and this was the only way to do it.

Marnie had leapt off of cliffs so many times that first year, following her mother down the faces of the canyons.

Rescuing her. Helping her back up. Only to have to dive off the cliff and go save her again.

Then all those months of searching for her mother, plunging off cliff after cliff.

It made her sick at heart. She couldn't do it anymore.

So she didn't. Ever. Not once she gave up on finding her mother's body.

Marnie decided never to fall into flight again.

But that was a long time ago. Her life was different now.

Marnie wanted her life to be different.

So she stood on the brink of a snow-laden cliff, held out her arms, and launched herself forward.

The initial plunge used to thrill her when she was young.

Now she fought back the bile in her throat.

She allowed herself to fall only a few feet before she paddled her arms hard against the cold air.

Then she was soaring again, sailing along with the current.

She turned toward another cliff, and made herself do it again.

Her only consolation was that she would make a game of doing inside the hangar, too, but she would add the enjoyment of getting better at piloting the transports.

Christopher, true to the promise he had made her when she first arrived, had offered to show Marnie how to control the transports.

There were several of them lined up on the left wall of the hangar, all with the strange-looking circlets draped over a peg at the front of the craft.

"One size fits all," Christopher said, as he slipped the headband over his head. Small white lights lit up all down the band.

"I'm going to think now," he said. *"Lift a foot off the floor."* Then he closed his mouth and didn't speak again.

A moment later, the transport lifted vertically off the floor and hovered a foot above it.

Then it lowered back to the ground, and Christopher took off the headband and gave it to Marnie.

"You try. It's a little strange at first, but once you get used to it, you're gonna love it."

Marnie settled the headband across her forehead and down over the top of her ears. Christopher's head looked bigger than hers with his thick black hair, but he was right, the headband fit Marnie perfectly.

She stepped onto the base of the transport.

"So I just… tell it," she said.

"Or ask it," Christopher said. "Either way. You'll find your style."

Marnie closed her eyes and sent her thought to the transport. *I want to go high. But don't hit my head.*

The chariot-looking transport lifted Marnie smoothly upward to the top of the hangar.

It took her command literally, coming to a stop so close to the ceiling, she could only fit her hand in between it and the top of her head.

Down, she told it, and it descended at the same smooth rate as before. Marnie felt secure, not in danger of falling off.

"Think you have it?" Christopher asked her.

"Can I play around with it for a while?"

"Just stay out of the lane of the active pods," he said, pointing to where rows of them took turns bubbling up to the openings at the top of the hangar.

Marnie experimented with the transport for the next several hours, only stopping long enough to get in some flying to satisfy her urge.

She parked the transport, then ran and leapt into flight. She was still resisting the method she had used before. She could have risen on the transport all the way up toward the ceiling, then launched herself from there.

But she wasn't ready then. She wasn't even ready yesterday.

Marnie promised herself she would break through her mental barrier today, on the anniversary.

And now, after making herself dive off of ten cliffs in a row, she was ready to go back into the warmth of the hangar and play around with a transport.

She flew back to where she had stowed her coat, pants, and boots under the tree.

But somebody else was already there waiting.

4

"Hiya," Sharman said. She gave Marnie a small wave.

"H-hi." Marnie gave her an uncertain wave back.

She glanced around her, like there might be more people hiding someplace else.

Sharman couldn't blame her for her confusion. Sharman had popped the lid of her pod and still sat inside it, making only the upper half of her body visible to Marnie's eyes.

Sharman reached down to the sides of the pod and pulled out her ankle-high boots. She put them on.

She climbed out of the pod, wishing she had thought to bring a coat out here, too. Her flight suit was warm, but not warm enough.

She held out her hand. "Sharman Hix."

Marnie shook it and introduced herself.

"You're the pilot," Marnie said, then she rolled her eyes. "Of course you're the pilot…"

Sharman grinned. "Far as I'm concerned, can't hear that enough."

She wrapped her arms around her chest. "Mind if I wear your coat? I'm a little underdressed."

"Uh… sure," Marnie said, and even though she had been about to put it on, she handed it to Sharman instead.

Sharman wrapped herself inside it. Marnie was about half a foot taller, so the coat hung long.

"Wanna try it?" Sharman asked Marnie, motioning toward the pod. "I'll put the lid over you. You'll be nice and warm."

"How did you… how did you know I was here?" Marnie asked. "I thought no one could see me when I flew."

"We're made of the same thing," Sharman said. "My ship and your suit. All the pods can see each other. I can see you, too."

"Have you been flying out there?" Marnie asked.

"Uh-huh."

"I never saw you."

Sharman shrugged. "You have to learn how to look."

She motioned again toward the seat inside her pod.

Marnie hesitated, but then she accepted the invitation.

It was like the headband, she discovered. The pod seemed to adjust to her size. The foot pedestal moved down. The arms of the chair extended longer.

Sharman still wore her lighted white headband, but she fished out another from the side of the pod and fitted it around Marnie's head, over the top of her flight suit's hood. Marnie could feel the headband hum.

"Think you can do it?" Sharman asked.

"What, fly this?" Marnie said. Her face suddenly paled. Sharman laughed.

"I saw you with the transport the other day," Sharman said. "You're a natural. Pods are the same thing. Just talk to them. Hear them back."

Sharman touched the back of the domed lid and it began rising over Marnie's head.

"Wait!" Marnie said.

Sharman tapped the side of her own lighted band and said, "Training wheels. I got ya."

Once the lid sealed shut, Sharman gave Marnie a thumbs-up and mouthed, *You can do this.*

Marnie closed her eyes. Her heart hammered in her chest.

But from excitement as much as from fear.

The pod felt like a cocoon, made especially for Marnie. A pale cream color inside, soothing to her eyes.

There were no instruments. No dials or lights or displays.

Just the view outside through the clear domed window.

The arms of the chair felt warm against the sleeves of Marnie's suit. It felt even warmer underneath her extended fingers.

There were small indentations there that seemed perfectly fitted to the shape of her fingertips.

The whole chair molded around her. She felt comfortable rather than confined.

The ribbed footpads of her suit slipped into indentations on the platform raised from the floor. Marnie's feet were much bigger than Sharman's, but once again, it was a perfect fit.

Sharman knocked on the lid of the pod. "Freezing out here! Get up and go!"

Marnie took a deep breath.

It's just like the transport.

Talk to them. Hear them back.

"*Up,*" Marnie told the pod with her mind.

The craft lifted her off of the ground.

Could she risk it? She wasn't afraid of heights or of flight.

But that was because she was in complete control whenever she flew.

Now she was trapped inside this bubble, looking out through its domed window, and there were no brakes, no controls of any kind.

She was the control.

A slow smile spread across Marnie's face.

She turned to Sharman and gave her a thumbs-up back.

"Let's go," she told the pod, and it flew her out across the snow, following the exact path of Marnie's first takeoff this morning, the one she started from a run.

It was so much faster than the transport, it took her breath away.

She was really flying, not gliding at that safe, slow pace.

But after a few minutes the speed didn't frighten her anymore.

And the height and the looming mountainsides didn't bother her, either. Marnie had already flown all of these same skies for the past few hours.

She settled in. She soon felt like she understood the rules. How to think, what to tell it, how to move it.

It was flight of a different kind, and she knew it wouldn't be enough when the need returned, any more than a runner could get her runner's high just by driving a fast car.

But it filled a space in Marnie's troubled heart that she didn't realize needed this to fill it.

She coaxed the pod higher. And higher. Higher than Marnie normally flew. The craft shuddered in the cold and changeable current, but Marnie kept going.

She had almost reached a bank of dark clouds when she lost her nerve, and thought that was high enough.

But she didn't panic. She told the pod it was time to go back. Sharman must be cold. They needed to go inside.

Marnie guided the pod back to a smooth and soft landing.

Sharman looked up from a small screen she held in one hand while the other hand stayed buried in the pocket of Marnie's coat.

Sharman stowed the screen in the top of her left ankle-high boot. She stood waiting for Marnie to pop the top.

The lid of the pod slid silently over and behind Marnie's head.

"What did you think?" Sharman asked, smiling. She offered her hand and helped Marnie climb out.

"Good," Marnie said, "but now I have to fly some. My way. Work off some of the adrenaline."

Sharman nodded. "Understood."

She handed the coat back to Marnie, then climbed back inside her pod. Marnie returned the borrowed headband.

She could imagine everything inside the pod readjusting to Sharman's smaller size.

"I knew you could do it," Sharman said. "Like I said, you're a natural. I'll teach you, if you want to learn."

Marnie wrapped the down coat around her. She felt cold, just standing in the wind.

"Why?" Marnie asked.

Sharman laughed. "Why? Because you kick ass at it, that's why."

"What… what am I supposed to do with it?"

What are you trying to make me do? was what Marnie meant.

This was it, exactly what she had been expecting to happen.

What they wanted from her.

How she was supposed to pay.

These were the feds, after all, even Major Zimholt.

Nobody gave anything for free.

Her mother had warned her that from the start.

Marnie had been so close to believing. So close to letting down her guard.

But Alice would be proud of her now.

Sharman must have forgotten about wearing the headband.

Training wheels.

Must not have realized that Marnie could hear her.

When the call came in through that screen Marnie saw Sharman holding, Marnie heard every word.

"Will she do it?" asked Major Zimholt.

Sharman laughed. "Oh, she'll do it."

"Did you tell her?"

Sharman: "No, should I?"

Major Zimholt: "No. She doesn't need to know."

Sharman: "Gotta go. She's coming back."

The call ended. Marnie's heart fell to her stomach.

Cold sweat broke out on her forehead. Her palms felt slick against the arms of the chair.

What an idiot she had been.

Idiot, juvenile, fantasizing that Major Zimholt was her long-lost grandfather.

Fantasizing that she was safe here, or anywhere else.

Should she leave right now? Just go?

What about Alice? Should she go back to her first and warn her?

Was Alice safe here? Was it just Marnie that they wanted?

If Marnie played along, would they protect Alice?

Or should both of them leave as soon as they could?

Because she did believe in Alice. She had to. In her honesty, in her friendship.

Marnie wasn't that stupid, although right now she felt ashamed of how easily she had been seduced.

Giving her a friendly wave, Sharman lifted her pod into the air and shot off toward what Marnie assumed was the roof of the hangar. She had seen pods come in, just as she saw them bubble up and out through the ceiling. Sharman had accomplished whatever they sent her out here to do.

Marnie was so tired of running. But it had been this way for so long, she barely remembered any other way to live.

January 4, twelve years ago, was the end of her natural life.

She was an alien, not from the future or any advanced race, just *other*, and it was never going to change.

But she wouldn't be turned into something else she didn't want.

Once was enough. She wouldn't let it happen again.

Marnie walked to the edge of the cliff and looked down.

She shucked off the coat and let it fall to the snow.

She spread out her arms and took flight. The air felt cold and wet. It was going to snow again soon, she could feel it.

If there were pods out here with her, the pilots watching her, Marnie didn't know how to see them.

She wished now that she had kept going. That she had flown the pod higher and higher into the clouds.

Higher still, toward the black starry heavens.

Higher still, into outer space.

To where some distant, unknown galaxy might embrace her and take her in. Swallow her into the light of its own sun and stars.

But that chance was gone. And Marnie doubted that it would ever come again.

She had faltered, given in to fear, and now she was stuck here with life as it was.

Marnie had to accept that.

Just as she had to accept so many other things about this life that she never chose for herself.

Marnie stifled a cry, strangled it inside her throat. She

wouldn't give in to the sorrow that wanted to overtake her. If she did, she knew that she was lost.

She would search for someplace new and begin again, just as she had so many times before.

Alice was smart and tough—tougher than Marnie could ever be. Alice would take care of herself.

Marnie snapped her mind to the task at hand as she pumped her thin arms through the cold snowy air.

Watched, by something not entirely human.

Next in the Dove Season Universe
SEEKER

- UFO biologist Dr. Travis Baird investigates a new species of alien in the Arizona desert. Friend or foe? He's about to find out.
- Marnie Stemple has a power that other people want. The only way to stay safe from capture is to keep running. Or is there another way?
- Pilot Sharman Hix fights to communicate with her experimental aircraft before it crashes. How can she get through to it in time?
- Agency analyst Alice Kern continues to search for the answers behind her parents' murder. But is she really ready to hear the truth?
- Scientist-soldier Julie Trident investigates a violent species of alien. What she discovers may change the way humans do battle against them.

The truth is out there. Whether we're ready for it or not.

ABOUT THE AUTHOR

Robin Brande is an award-winning author, former trial attorney, black belt in martial arts, Reiki Master, and wilderness medic. Her outdoor adventures range from the Rocky Mountains to the Alps to Iceland.

She writes in multiple genres, including mystery, adventure, fantasy, science fiction, young adult, romance, and self-help.

For more information:
https://robinbrande.com/

For updates about upcoming installments of DOVE SEASON, along with previews and special discounts, subscribe to the Robin Brande newsletter: https://robinbrande.com/pages/subscribe.

MORE FROM ROBIN BRANDE

SHOW YOUR BOOK-LOVING STYLE!

AND SCIENCE LOVING, ART LOVING, DOG AND CAT LOVING, AND MORE...

Treat yourself to a soft, comfy, custom-made T-shirt designed by Robin Brande herself, inspired by her own books. You can see all of them at robinbrande.com/collections/t-shirts.

And here's a secret just for you: Use the discount code **READER10** at checkout to get **10% off any items in the store**. That means books, T-shirts, hoodies, mugs—whatever you'd like. Go ahead and treat yourself, book lover.

CERTIFIED
BOOK NERD
WORTH IT, NERD
CERTIFIED
DOG NERD
NERDS FTW
CERTIFIED
SCIENCE NERD

books
every
day
Sleep enough
Eat enough
FIRST TWO RULES of
Adventure
SLEEP ENOUGH
EAT ENOUGH

Retired psychology professor Dr. Winifred Parsons spent decades studying the human psyche as a scientist and academic. But she also explored it from another angle: Winnie Parsons is clairvoyant.

Now Winnie uses her psi talent to help clients resolve mysteries that are outside the reach of standard investigations.

The path to justice might be twisted, but Winnie always finds a way.

Life after death, miracle healings, communication with other species...

- *The Water Healers*: A nurse investigates rumors of miracle healers in Mexico.
- *A Drop of Sweat*: A clairvoyant secretly uses her skills to unravel the mystery of who destroyed a scientist's lab.
- *The Refugees*: A volunteer helps the refugees fleeing a planetary disaster.
- *The Bridge*: A grieving widow refuses to believe her husband is gone forever.
- *The Outpost Away from the World*: A scientist returns to the off-the-grid cabin of her childhood and discovers the mysterious secret to her survival.

The mountains can dish it out. But that doesn't mean you have to take it.

- *On Red Mountain*: A woman must survive alone in the mountains after her husband is struck by lightning.
- *The Rescue*: A mountain hermit and his dog race to avert a coming disaster—one that the dog senses before anyone else.
- *Home Deer*: A mountain widow takes matters into her own hands to protect the nearby woodland creatures.
- *The Gold Hunter*: An injured climber's only hope for survival is a stranger who won't give up.
- *Taken at Rustler Pass*: A teen girl fights to survive against the stranger who wants her dead.

High school senior and amateur physicist Audie Masters discovers a parallel universe—along with a parallel version of herself.

It's the adventure of a lifetime.

Now all she has to do is survive it.

Read all four books in the exciting, mind-bending PARALLELO-GRAM QUARTET. You'll never look at the universe or your own life the same way again.